WHITE CHRISTMAS WITH A WOBBLY KNEE

A Lady Amanda Golightly Murder Mystery

The Belchester Chronicles: Book Two

ANDREA FRAZER

Other books by Andrea Frazer

The Belchester Chronicles

Strangeways to Oldham
Snowballs and Scotch Mist
Old Moorhen's Shredded Sporran

The Falconer Files

Death of an Old Git
Choked Off
Inkier than the Sword
Pascal Passion
Murder at the Manse
Music to Die For
Strict and Peculiar
Christmas Mourning
Grave Stones
Death in High Circles
Glass House

The Falconer Files – Brief Cases

Love Me To Death
A Sidecar Named Expire
Battered to Death
Toxic Gossip
Driven to It
All Hallows
Death of a Pantomime Cow

Others

Choral Mayhem

DRAMATIS PERSONAE

RESIDENT AT BELCHESTER TOWERS

Lady Amanda Golightly – owner
Hugo Cholmondley-Crichton-Crump – her old friend
Beauchamp – manservant and general factotum
Lady Edith Golightly – mother of Lady Amanda, and presumed dead for twenty years

GUESTS

Colonel Henry and Mrs Hilda Heyhoe-Caramac – aka Bonkers and Fluffy
Sir Jolyon and Lady Felicity *ff*olliat DeWinter – aka Blimp and Fifi
Major Montgomery and Mrs Madeleine Mapperley-Minto aka Monty and Maddie
Captain Leslie and Mrs Lesley Barrington-Blyss – aka Popeye and Porky
Sir Montacute and Lady Margaret Fotherington-Flint – aka Cutie and Daisy
Lt Col. Aloysius & Mrs Angelica Featherstonehaugh-Armitage – aka Stinky and Donkey

OTHERS

Enid Tweedie – domestic and occasional waitress
Dr Anstruther – an elderly GP
Dr Campbell Andrew – a younger GP
Sundry domestics, etc.

POLICE

Detective Inspector Moody – of the Belchester CID
Police Constable Glenister – of the Belchester Police

Author's note on pronunciation of names

'**Beauchamp**' is a fine French name, but in England is pronounced 'Beecham' by all, with the notable exception of Lady Amanda, who insists on the French pronunciation.

'**Cholmondley-Crichton**' is pronounced 'Chumley-Cryton'.

'**Featherstonehaugh**' is pronounced 'Fanshaw'.

'**Bradshaigh**' is pronounced 'Bradshaw'.

Someone really ought to tell Enid Tweedie! She thought she could read English!

Prologue
A Rave from the Grave

The very old lady made herself comfortable in a wing-backed chair, raised her glass, and proposed a toast. 'To the return of the prodigal!' she said, and swallowed her champagne cocktail in one gulp. 'I'll have another, if you please, Beauchamp,' she said, imperiously, handing her glass to the unperturbed manservant.

'Yes, my lady,' he intoned, taking the glass, and making to walk away.

'Hang on, Beauchamp, we have something to sort out here with regard to modes of address. I suggest that, while I'm here, you address me as "your ladyship", and my daughter as "my lady". That should sort out any misunderstandings before they happen.'

Lady Amanda, her hand raised to her cheeks with shock, her eyes staring, said, 'But, Mummy, you've been dead these twenty years. How on earth can you be here? You died in that car crash with Daddy, or am I losing my mind?'

Lady Edith and her husband had been killed in a car accident on the London to Brighton Rally some twenty or so years ago, or so everybody had believed at the time, and Amanda had become Lady Amanda, and chatelaine of Belchester Towers.

Belchester Towers had been in her family since it was built by one of her forefathers. in the early nineteenth century. It was a red-brick structure in the likeness of a castle, even having a moat and drawbridge in its early years, before everything got too difficult with deliveries

1

and the advent of the motor car.

Lady Amanda had taken it over happily, running her estate with only the help of her manservant and general factotum, Beauchamp, and the occasional help of an army of people from nearby Belchester, who came in periodically to give the place a 'good going over'. Beauchamp arranged all this, as he did keeping the grounds mowed and clipped, and in a respectable condition.

The only regular help had been a woman from the windy backstreets of Belchester, by the name of Enid Tweedie, who had become very attached to Lady Amanda, a real friend in times of trouble. And, of trouble, there had been plenty in the recent past. Lady Amanda had not only discovered her old friend Hugo, mouldering away in a Belchester nursing home, but also another old friend, freshly despatched to the Almighty, and by human hand.

The subsequent events, which included getting Hugo moved into Belchester Towers, seeing a proper doctor, instead of the bumbling old fool he had been consulting, the ramifications of the murder, and their investigation into it, had changed her life beyond recognition.

And now, here was Lady Amanda's supposedly long-dead mother, actually back in her old surroundings, taking over the situation, as she always had done in life. What had Lady Amanda done to deserve this, she wondered, still unable to believe that this was not a nightmare from which she would soon awake, and laugh off, in the light of day. She waited, in complete disbelief, for her mother's explanation of how events were now flowing, and apparently had been, these last two decades.

'Oh, Manda,' her mother replied, completely unruffled, 'you always were naive and gullible. Somebody died in that car crash, but it certainly wasn't me; was it, Beauchamp?' she added.

'No, your ladyship,' confirmed Beauchamp, without

turning a hair.

'You mean you knew about this, Beauchamp: and you never uttered a word to me about it, in all this time?'

'That is correct, my lady,' replied Beauchamp, his face a blank.

'How could you! And just exactly who *did* die in that car, then, because they certainly buried somebody, and everyone – with the exception of secretive old Beauchamp here – thought it was you. I'm losing my mind – I know I am. This is all an hallucination, and I shall wake up in the nut-hut!'

'That was my personal maid, Manda. Didn't you notice how furtive she and Daddy were, when they were in the same room together. They were always sneaking off, too. Oh, I knew they were having an affair. That's why I ran away during the night, before the day of the rally. I'd got wind of the fact – thank you very much for that, Beauchamp – that they were going to run away together on that rally, and I wasn't going to be stuck here, with only that ghastly county set for company.'

'So where have you been all this time?'

'Why, the Riviera, of course, Manda. I'd already salted away a great deal of money on the continent, and I just needed to get out with some of my clothes and my jewels. Your father didn't even notice I'd gone, I'm sure. We had separate bedrooms, after all. I just got someone to drive me to the station in the middle of the night, and I had all my arrangements made by letter and telephone, for the other end. By the way, thank you again, Beauchamp, for your part as secret chauffeur.'

'I simply don't believe this!' Lady Amanda was incensed. 'My own mother and my own manservant, in cahoots, deceiving me for two decades, and I suspected nothing.'

'Well, least said, soonest mended,' commented her mother, playing a new tune on an old saw.

'And, no doubt you'll expect to be known as Lady Edith again?' Manda was catching on fast.

'Well, it is my name, and I'm entitled to use it, as the dowager, now your father's dead.'

'And where exactly does that leave me?' (There may be trouble ahead – cue violins!)

'In just the same place that you are now, and have been for the last twenty years,' said the dowager, giving her daughter the ghost of a smile. She might have known that her daughter's first thought would have been for her own position.

'Well, that's all right then. But how long are you planning to stay? You're not moving in for ever, are you?' Thus, Lady Amanda betrayed feelings it would have been better to suppress, but Lady Edith was a thick-skinned woman, and just ignored the slight.

'Only until they've finished renovating my new apartment in Monte Carlo. I've recently moved, you know. It'll only be a few weeks – a few months, at the most.'

Lady Amanda didn't know whether to be relieved or horrified. How would she cope with her mother back here, and no doubt trying to run her life for her again? She must be as old as the hills. What right had she to turn up here from the grave and look so sprightly?

'I think you'd better make that three – no, four – more champagne cocktails, Beauchamp. And tell me, why does Manda insist on calling you Beauchamp? I never did.'

'No, your ladyship, but your husband always insisted on the French pronunciation, so I suppose she just carried on the paternal tradition.'

'Stuff and nonsense. Now, fetch those drinks, there's a good man, before I die of thirst!'

Lady Amanda was sorely tempted by this remark, but with an enormous effort of will, managed to keep her thoughts to herself.

'It's good to see you again, Lady Edith.' Hugo spoke

for the first time since Lady Amanda had opened the front door and been confronted with what she at first thought was the shade of her mother. 'I always enjoyed my visits to Belchester Towers.'

'You're here rather late, though, aren't you? When are you going home?' Lady Edith was even more forthright than her daughter, and wasted no time on small talk.

Hugo looked pointedly at Lady Amanda, considering that it should be she who explained the current situation to her mother. 'Hugo lives here now, Mummy,' she said, but got no further.

'What, you two, living "over the brush" at your time of life? You should be ashamed of yourselves.'

This really made her daughter bristle. 'It's nothing like that, Mummy, and I'd have thought you'd have known better than to suggest such a thing. I found Hugo marooned in the most ghastly nursing home, because the arthritis in his hips and knees had got so bad, he couldn't manage at home on his own.

'I rescued him, and brought him here, and he's seen my own doctor, and has had his first appointment with the orthopaedic consultant at the hospital. Hugo and I are platonic friends; have never been, and never will be, anything else.'

'Good girl! Now, have we still got that old Carstairs invalid chair? I shall enjoy the grounds once more, if I can press one of you to take me out in it. And, I can be a little hard of hearing. Is Great-grandmama's ear-trumpet still up in the attics? I'll get Beauchamp to fetch it for me. The battery's gone in my hearing aid, and I'll need something to get me through until I can send you on an errand to fetch me some new ones. Still got my old trikes, have you?'

'Of course, we have, Mummy. I use the black one, and I've been teaching Hugo to ride your red one. I even got *Beauchamp*,' (she pronounce the name with the greatest of emphasis), 'to transfer the motor from Daddy's bicycle to it, and make the necessary alterations.

'*Beauchamp* has also got the old lift working again, so you can have your old room back, on the first floor.'

Beauchamp returned, at this juncture, bearing a freshly laden tray, and Hugo cried out, 'Cocktail time, everybody!'

Chapter One
Settling-in Spats and Other Arguments

Beauchamp made up Lady Edith's bed and prepared her room for her and, after she had creaked her way upstairs in the lift, Lady Amanda and Hugo were left alone together, to contemplate their drastically altered immediate future.

'I don't know how I'm going to cope with her bossiness and interference again,' complained Lady Amanda.

'I know how you feel,' agreed Hugo, but not exactly thinking of those qualities in Lady Edith.

'What am I going to do, Hugo, old thing?' she wailed.

'You've always got me,' Hugo reassured her.

'Yes,' she replied, then sighed heavily. 'I know!'

There were, of course, uncomfortable moments, in this settling-down period.

'It's 'Beauchamp!' pronounced Lady Amanda, with fervour.

'No, it's not. It's 'Beecham'!' argued Lady Edith, with fervour.

'Beauchamp!'

'Beecham!'

'Beauchamp!'

'Beecham. Why do you persist with this ridiculous French pronunciation?' asked Lady Edith, her hackles rising.

'Because Daddy always called him "Beauchamp"!' Lady Amanda's hackles could rise too, and hers were years younger than her mother's.

'Beecham!'

'Beauchamp!'

'Beecham!'

'Yes, my ladies?' replied that named individual, appearing as if by magic by their sides.

'Bugger!' swore Lady Amanda, uncharacteristically, and stomped off to her room to sulk.

'I don't see how you can be standing there, so obviously alive, when I've got your Death Certificate in my bureau.'

'Not worth the paper it's written on!' replied her mother, stubbornly.

'I've still got it, and you'd better watch out, or I might just shop you to the fuzz.'

'Don't use such appalling slang, girl! I'll simply tell them that I remembered nothing since the accident, until recently, suffering from amnesia for all these years, as I have.'

'You wouldn't dare!'

'Just you try me, my girl!'

'How are you going to explain to the Queen that she'll have to send a telegram to a long-dead woman, in a few years' time? She'll probably stick you in the Tower.'

'I shall say that rumours of my death were somewhat exaggerated, but that I'm feeling much better now, thank you.'

'Oh, Mummy, you are absolutely impossible!'

'But you've *got* to go, Mummy. I've got my *own* life to live now that you're dead. And if you don't take yourself back off to the Continent, I shall make public, the fact that you ran a knocking shop here for the American servicemen, during the war. And I shall tell about Daddy and his Black Market deals. And what if it were to be made known that he had worked as an arms dealer after the War? What would people say to that? If all your secrets came out, apart from the fact that you're simply not DEAD, where would you be?' Lady Amanda was furious, and having one of her tantrums.

'I should be a frail old lady with memory loss, or, if I fled, simply a figment of your imagination. You, however, should all this get to official ears, would be stripped of your title, and I'm sure the tax office would be more than happy to strip your comfortable bank account as well, to cover all the unpaid taxes from Daddy's and my illegal activities. Now, how do you like *them* potatoes?' Lady Edith smiled angelically at her daughter, then licked her right index finger, and drew a vertical line in the air.

'My house-point, I rather think, my dear!'

'I just can't stand it any more, Hugo. Every time someone comes to the house, I have to shove Mama behind a door or into a cupboard, in case someone sees her and rumbles what's going on up here. She seems to think it's a hoot, but it's playing merry hell with my nerves. My life seems to be one endless game of 'Hunt the Slipper', with Mama being the slipper: and she's got wheels too. What if she thinks it's a jolly jape to wheel herself out into open view? The gaff will be well and truly blown, and we shall all end up in gaol – except you, of course – with a list of charges against us as long as your arm. I just can't stand the tension: I'm permanently on an adrenalin overload.'

'May I suggest more cocktails,' suggested Hugo, considering this idea with his head cocked to one side. 'It won't alter the situation at all, of course, but it will probably reduce your ability to fret over it, and give you a calmer and more relaxed view of things.'

'What? And let my mother turn me into a raging alcoholic?' She thought for a moment, then declared, 'Well, just until she goes, I suppose it's not a bad idea. Good man, Hugo! Have a Grasshopper! BEAUCHaaargh!

Dear God, man, my nerves are in shreds already. For the love of all that's holy, would you please not sneak up on me like that. In my current condition I'm liable to have a heart attack, and then where would your job be? Answer me that one! '

'I shall need a bit of cash before I go. You know how expensive moving ... Of course you don't! You've never lived anywhere but here, but I can assure you, it's a very costly business, and I could do with a bit of a top-up, if you'd be so kind,' Lady Edith asked, one day after afternoon tea.

Delighted at the thought of seeing the back of her mother, Lady Amanda asked how much she required, while Hugo looked on with keen interest.

'About a million should do it, I think. For now,' replied the ancient dowager.

Hugo's mouth fell open with amazement and horror. How on earth she could have the brass-necked cheek, after all these years of being dead, to ask her daughter for such an enormous amount of money, he had no idea.

'I'll just get my cheque book, and I'll give the old boy at the bank a call in the morning, to let him know that I'm authorising that sum to leave my account,' said Lady Amanda, and went off, in pursuit of her cheque book, calling back, 'You'll have to tell me who to make it out to, as I haven't the faintest idea under what crass alias you have been living these past twenty years.'

Hugo hadn't realised that his mouth could open any further, but it did, making him think that if he had another shock, while in this state, his chin might, literally, hit the floor.

Chapter Two
Problems with Workmen and Post-operation
Blues

Hugo's first hip replacement operation had taken place in the autumn. Lady Edith had got her feet well under the table by then and, when Lady Amanda had enquired, as politely as she could, when they would be seeing the back of the old bird, she was always ready with some excuse; for example, 'The plumber's on holiday for three weeks, and the electrician can't get on with his work until the plumber comes back,' or 'The plasterer's in Paris on an urgent job, and he'll be gone for at least a month.'

'You seem to suffer from an awful lot of bad luck with your workmen, Mummy,' Lady Amanda had commented sourly, but to the old lady it was just like water off a duck's back. Her daughter was taking things remarkably well, publicly, considering that, only a few short months ago, she had been 'Queen of the Shit Heap', as Lady Edith coarsely described it, and here she was now, back under her mother's eagle eye, and with Hugo twittering at her all the time; but her outward patience wouldn't last for ever.

The priority at the moment, however, was Hugo. Having just been discharged from hospital within only days of his surgery ('We need the beds, sir.') there were certain delicate problems to be sorted out, with regard to his mobility, while he recuperated.

Social Services had kindly sent round a commode for Hugo's use, and it was this that had caused the current outburst of rebellion: that, and the metal crutches that had arrived with it.

'I am NOT using that thing!' Hugo had never expressed himself with such volume and anger before, and he pointed at the object of his anger, the commode, as he shouted. 'I will not have THAT THING in my bedroom, with its potty sticking out through the seat for all to see. I may be old, but I insist on retaining my dignity.'

Wading in, with her fingers crossed behind her back for luck, Lady Amanda made a suggestion. 'We have a very old commode in the attic. It just looks like a cube of carved wood – a bit like a large, ornate box. Nobody would ever guess it was a commode.'

'That sounds more acceptable, but I'll have to see it first,' replied Hugo, slightly mollified, and hoping that, as usual, Lady Amanda would come to his rescue.

'I'll get Beauchamp to fetch it down for you,' she soothed him.

'And I'm not walking with those blasted things, either,' said Hugo, pointing to the crutches.

'Why ever not?' she asked.

'Because they'll make me look like a silly old man, who's fallen over and injured himself. I will not go round looking like a victim of my age! And that's final! I had enough of that with that damned Zimmer frame.'

'Beau …'

'Already here, my lady.' Beauchamp spoke quietly from just behind her right shoulder.

'Oh, you did give me a fright! I've told you not to creep around like that. It's very unnerving.'

'Yes, my lady. How can I be of assistance?'

'Firstly, you can fetch down the carved commode from the attics, and secondly, have you still got that rack of walking canes in your pantry?'

'I have, indeed, my lady,' the manservant answered.

'Then perhaps you could fetch them along, too? The commode is for Hugo's bedroom, and the walking canes can be brought here, for his inspection. He doesn't like the utilitarian crutches, and would like something a little less "medical" to aid his walking.'

'Very good, my lady.'

Beauchamp really was a peach of an asset to the household, thought Lady Amanda, as he left them to carry out his errand.

A little later, Hugo inspected the many fine walking canes available for his use, with enthusiasm. He'd already okayed the 'po', as Lady Edith vulgarly put it, and was now choosing the canes he would like to 'test-walk'.

'I really like this one, with the silver greyhound's head on it. It's just the right height, it's as straight as a die, and it holds well.'

As he went through the sticks, Lady Edith, who had joined them when she heard Beauchamp transferring them into the drawing room, was giving a running commentary on to whom they had belonged in the past.

'That one was Great Uncle Wilbur's. He used to love going to the dog track. Terrible gambler, you know. Just as well my Jonathan came along when he did in the family. Where would the family fortunes be, if it wasn't for Golightly's Health Products?'

'Oh, shut up, Mummy, for goodness' sake, and let Hugo get on with choosing.' It was amazing how the presence of her mother could turn a woman of her age into the petulant child she once had been.

Hugo now selected one with the head of a bulldog: ivory, with ruby eyes. 'I say, this one's a really fine thing. I think I could cut quite a dash, out and about with this in my hand,' he crowed, examining it for damage and suitability.

'That one was Grandpa Golightly's – your father's father's, Manda, dear,' Lady Edith crowed, delighted to see such an old friend again. 'He bred bulldogs.'

'How do you know it's his? He was already dead when

you married Daddy.' Lady Amanda was getting herself into a grand sulk.

'Because your father told me so, my dearest,' replied her mother, with the sweetest of smiles, guaranteed to annoy her daughter, and get under her skin.

'Oh, I've had enough of this! I'm going off to do something else. The sticks are usually in the butler's pantry, should you wish to change either of them, Hugo. I'll just leave you to it with Mummy dearest.'

Chapter Three
New Horizons

Over the period of his convalescence and beyond, Hugo constantly suggested to Lady Amanda that she open up part of the house to the public. He knew she didn't need the money, but she did need something to take her interest – something that she could get her teeth into, and keep both her mind and her body active. Her mother was driving her to distraction, and she had too little to do.

After all the change, with Hugo moving in, and working on solving murders, life, with the exception of the prickle in her side that was her female parent, had settled down to a gnawing boredom.

'Why don't we get this place spruced up a bit – just some of it, you know – and we could do little tours for the public. Someone could take them round the bits you've selected, and give them the history of the place and the Golightly family, and perhaps we could serve cream teas as well; let them walk round the grounds, that sort of thing, don't yer know?' he suggested, one morning after breakfast, when Lady Edith requested that her repast should be served on a tray in her room.

'What?' replied Lady Amanda. 'Fill the place with light-fingered plebs, you mean?'

'Of course not, Manda. If you charge a decent fee for admission, then the plebs won't want to pay to come and look around. If you can manage the guided tours yourself, you could ask a good whack, what with you having a title and everything. It'll give you a purpose in life.'

'I wasn't aware that I needed a purpose in my life,

Hugo. What makes you think I do?'

'Well, for one thing, your mother's driving you crazy. You could explain to her that, if she's still here when the tours start, she'll have to keep herself well-hidden, in case someone sees her and recognises her. It's all right her swanning around the Riviera and Monaco. She's unlikely to meet anyone from round here, there, and even if she did, she'd be able to pass it off as a case of mistaken identity.

'If anyone saw her in Belchester Towers itself, she'd have no defence. There's no coincidence that great, that her double should be staying here, so long after your mother's death. She has to remember that she is one of the dear departed, in local eyes, and she has to stay that way until her apartment's ready, and she can go off and leave us in peace.'

'You've certainly got a point there, Hugo. I believe the idea is beginning to grow on me,' she told him. 'Let's have a toddle round the place this morning, and see which bits could be tickled up to show to the paying public. Yes, I'm definitely warming to the idea. When do you think we could be ready?'

'We'll have to see how much needs to be done first, and how much of the place you're willing to show off,' Hugo advised her, not wanting her to make any hasty decisions that would leave them with too much to do, and too little time in which to do it.

'Good idea, old stick! The only thing that would be more fun would be another murder,'

'Heaven forbid!' replied Hugo.

But the gods don't like to be challenged, and can be quite contrary, should they feel in the mood to meddle in human affairs.

Their own personal tour of the house rewarded them with much useful information for their proposed venture into the tourist industry. The structure of the building had been

16

kept in good fettle by Lady Amanda, during her reign here, and there was no visible damp.

'That's the benefit of the place not being a thousand years old,' she told him, as they walked round. 'This was only built two hundred years ago, and I believe no expense was spared in making it impervious to the invasion of damp and general mould. Daddy also did a lot of work when there was a problem in the banqueting hall, and he always kept the roof in good repair, as have I. In fact, it was Daddy who put this family back on its feet again, but I'll tell you about that some other time.'

Getting back to the subject of the house, Hugo said, happily, 'There's quite a lot you could show then, with the removal of the dust sheets, and a bit of a clean-up.'

'There's actually too much of it to show, in my opinion. I'm absolutely exhausted,' moaned Lady Amanda, as they finally got back to the drawing room, and she could flop down into a chair to rest her feet.

'That's even better, Manda,' commented Hugo, cryptically.

'How is that better? My feet feel like they've been beaten for hours with sticks of bamboo.'

'You could have two or three different tours on offer, for different days, or different weeks. That way you could get people to come here two or three times, paying every time they come back.'

'Hugo, you're a right little entrepreneur, aren't you?'

'Thank you very much, Manda. It's very kind of you to say so.'

'What's that?' quavered a voice from a chair by the door, which they had not noticed was occupied.

'Oh, Mummy, you nearly frightened the life out of me. You're getting as bad a Beauchamp.'

'Beecham! And I couldn't help overhearing. What are you two up to? Anything exciting?' asked Lady Edith.

'Nothing that involves you, Mummy, or, in fact, could

involve you. I'm thinking of opening the house to the public, and we couldn't possibly risk you being seen alive, so you'll just have to keep out of the way whenever we do it, or I shall be compelled to murder you.'

'I say! That's jolly unfair, and not very like you, Manda. I'd have imagined you'd hate the idea of the general public swarming all over your family home, putting their sticky fingerprints all over everything, and nicking the bibelots.'

'Not at all, Mumsy. Hugo's suggested a way we can do it without having to suffer the hoi polloi, and you can just put up with it, or beetle off to your apartment in Monte Carlo, and leave us in peace.'

'That's no way to speak to your poor, aged mother, Manda!' Lady Edith chided her.

'Agreed! But then, I'm not speaking to my poor aged mother, am I? I'm speaking, instead, to my fairly well-off, and soon to be even better-off, *dead* mother and, believe me, that makes a huge difference.'

'That's right! Shut me away in the attics, with only bread and water to live on. Treat me like a prisoner in my own home. Children can be so cruel these days.' Lady Edith was really displaying a wealth of self-pity of which Lady Amanda would not have thought her capable, had she not remembered that her mother had once been part of the Belchester Players, an amateur dramatic group that used to put on plays now and again in the city's theatre.

'Well, yah, boo, and sucks to you!' exclaimed Lady Amanda, very childishly, and promptly left the room, in search of a cocktail, even though it wasn't yet lunchtime.

Enid Tweedie was summoned (of course!) for the preparations for opening the house, and was soon to be found under everyone's feet, with a mop and bucket, singing old Eurovision Song Contest numbers much too loudly, and dramatically out of tune.

This stalwart had worked for Lady Amanda for more years than she cared to count, first as a cleaner who came in to do 'the rough', now rather more in the role of Beauchamp: that of general factotum and friend of convenience. She never felt put upon by Lady Amanda, because she had been treated so well by her, during and after her many trips to hospital for minor operations. The latest one had been for ingrowing toenails, and she was only just back on her feet after that.

Lady Amanda spent the bulk of her time at the library table, covering it with a multitude of sheets of paper, planning the various tours that could be offered, and the commentary that would accompany the proposed guests round the various parts of the house.

Hugo, meanwhile, had had his second hip-replacement operation, and spent a lot of his time reading, with a little gentle exercise every now and then. He'd found some local history books in the library, sadly out of date, but, nonetheless, fascinating (for history tends not to change), and often spent his reading time in a porter's chair in the library, interrupting lady Amanda every few minutes, to read out something to her, or ask her opinion on an item he had just read.

Time passed, Mummy stayed on, like a barnacle on the bottom of a ship, and soon it was approaching December, the clocks gone back, and darkness falling slightly earlier every day, making their daily round almost dream-like. It was definitely time to make something happen to wake them all up, and get the wheels in motion for what they had been planning for months, now.

Even the thought of Christmas approaching could not really motivate Lady A. Life had become too predictable, and she was filled with ennui, wishing that something exciting would happen to liven things up again; not that she wished anyone dead, just to provide her with a murder to investigate. She was just hungry for a more dramatic side to her daily round – anything, to relieve the boredom that she felt she might not be able to shake off before the grave. In her opinion, life had been a bit too SOS (Same Old S**t) for some time now, and it was about time things livened up.

Chapter Four
Planning the Changes

'December, Manda!' exclaimed Hugo, over breakfast on the first of that month. 'If we don't do something soon, it'll be next year in no time at all.'

'I don't see what we can do at this time of year. No one will want to come out in this weather. It's freezing cold, dark, and miserable. I thought we'd probably open in the springtime,' she replied.

'But what about a rehearsal, just to get us in the mood.'

'A rehearsal? Whatever do you mean by that, Hugo?'

'Not sure! But give me this morning to think it over, and I'm sure to come up with something. I'll make some notes, and put it to you at cocktail time, when you're less likely to bite my head off.'

'I do not bite your head off, you old fake,' Lady Amanda denied, then, seeing the expression on her friend's face, flushed a little, and added, 'Well, not often, anyway.'

'There you go, then. We'll have a nice little natter over cocktails, this evening, and my head shall remain safe for the whole day.'

'Hugo!'

At six o'clock that evening, Hugo and Lady Amanda entered the drawing room to find it empty, and Beauchamp hot on their trail with a tray containing only two glasses. 'Where's Mummy?' enquired his employer, wishing her mother to Hell, for a nice little holiday. She should find plenty of like-minded people there that she would get on well with.

'Her ladyship is taking her cocktail and dinner in her room tonight. She has been busy all day, trying to finalise details of the completion of work on her new apartment, and is making haste to arrange travel plans,' replied the dignified Beauchamp.

Waiting until he was out of earshot, Lady A turned to Hugo, and punched a fist in the air. 'Thank goodness for that!' she said, with glee. 'The old witch is back off to the Continent!'

'Jolly D, Manda!' Hugo agreed with her, doing a little dance with his lower legs, as he sat in an armchair. 'Perhaps things can get back to something like normal now, with those murders over and done with, and your mother back amongst the living dead.'

'And we can get on with our plans to open up this place, so that it doesn't seem like quite such a mausoleum,' she suggested.

'I've been thinking about that,' declared Hugo, 'as I said I would this morning, and I believe I've got a jolly good idea for how to have a rehearsal, and spread the word amongst the "right sort" of people, who've always wanted to have a good nose round in here.'

'Shoot!' crowed Lady Amanda, necking her cocktail in one swallow, and ringing the bell to summon Beauchamp, so that she could have another celebratory swallow. She was feeling quite giddy with glee, at the thought of getting rid of her mother, and planned to make sure the giddiness could also be attributed to alcohol.

'They don't hunt any more round these parts, do they, after the ban and everything?' Hugo enquired.

'Oh, how I miss the thrill of the chase. How could they possibly have made it illegal?' wailed Lady Amanda, Hugo having accidentally provided her with one of her favourite soap boxes.

'But you said you hated all that horsey stuff with the

girls at school. I didn't know you rode,' Hugo said, perplexed. He clearly remembered her saying how she hated the way the girls were goofy about their ponies.

'That still stands. I couldn't be bothered with all that jumping over fences that were only six inches high, then getting a soppy rosette for it. And I still can't see the point of point-to-point. It's like having a racing car, and only ever driving it at thirty miles an hour.

'But hunting? That's a completely different kettle of horse-flesh. There's nothing like galloping across the countryside astride a fine hunter, sailing over fences and hedges, never knowing whether you're going to come a cropper. Now, that's real riding! And now, alas, it is no more,' she stated, with a tragic note in her voice.

'We did have a drag-hunt for a couple of years, but it just wasn't the same, so, now, we just don't bother. There is a Hunt Ball, but there's no Hunt as such, now. The MFH says it's not the same, now they can't tear an innocent animal to pieces at the end, so he's given up organising anything. And all the hounds have had to be euthanized. I bet people wouldn't be sniffy about hunting if they realised how many hounds had to be murdered, because there was no longer any use for them: but they don't think about that. It's all about the blasted verminous fox!

'So now the farmers have to shoot them, or trap them or use poison. It's taken a lot of the colourful history out of the countryside and, I think, made things worse for the fox, for they can shoot a darned sight more than they could have hunted, and I believe the poor things are having rather a thin time of it.

'I got rid of my hunter, you know, after last year's dreary drag-hunt. Christmas was tedious enough without Mummy and Daddy, but without the Hunt, it's going to be absolutely deathly.'

'Thanks for the potted history. A 'yes' or a 'no' would have sufficed,' scowled Hugo, who was getting a bit fed up with Lady A's mini-lectures. It seemed that he couldn't ask a straight question any more, and receive a straight answer. Everything came with embellishments.

'Why did you ask, then?' enquired Lady Amanda, now looking a little confrontational.

'Only because I've had the most marvellous idea, that won't only cheer up Christmas a good deal, but that could lead to us opening, and making a go of this place.'

'Continue,' was his companion's curt reply.

'Why don't we get the place freshly polished and dusted for the Season of Goodwill, which no doubt would have happened anyway, and invite some of the local nobs round on Boxing Day for a tour of the place and afternoon tea? That'll give you something to look forward to on the twenty-sixth, and take your mind of the fact that there's not even a drag-hunt for you to go galloping off on.

'There'd be no charge, of course, but we could let it be known, when they arrive, that we are trying out the idea which, if it gets good feedback, will be a reality in the spring. If they spread the word for us, we'll not only get the right sort of people, but it will be good for the area in general; bring more people into Belchester and the surrounding countryside.'

'What a topping idea, Hugo! You're a pocket genius, you are! And we've still got a few weeks to organise everything.' Lady Amanda was all smiles now. 'That would definitely give Boxing Day a bit of sparkle, rather than the anti-climax I was dreading.'

It was ages since she had entertained anyone but a few friends for cocktails or a cup of coffee or tea. The thought of having a gathering on Boxing Day seemed a sparkling idea to her. Christmas had been rather a dull affair ever since Mummy and Daddy had gone, and she felt a surge of enthusiasm for showing off the old place, decorated like it should be, and with a bit more life in it.

'And what about the old kitchen and scullery, and all

those other domestic offices? Beauchamp has a thoroughly modern kitchen. And I know he doesn't use the butler's pantry any more, because you keep all the silver in the strong-room', said Hugo, suddenly full of enthusiasm for this new idea.

'What about them? They're antediluvian, so they've all been shut up for donkey's years.'

'Exactly!' yelled Hugo, leaping, in slow motion, out of his chair in his excitement.

'Hugo, either I'm an idiot, or I can't see what you're seeing. Explain yourself.'

'That's all the go, these days, isn't? Looking back into the past, at how things used to be done. There're scads of programmes on the television about just that sort of thing. And what about collectors? They just love what I believe they call 'kitchen-alia'. You could work full-time just doing tours of the old domestic offices, and maybe the servants bedrooms – a "How They Used to Live" sort of tour. It would be a smash-hit! People would love it! And you could even let the plebs come in on that one, because it's not as if you're showing off the family jewels, is it?'

'Is this really true?' asked Lady Amanda, not really believing that people would pay good money to look at some old whisks and hair sieves.

'Of course it is, Manda. Give Enid a ring and ask her what she thinks about the idea, then you'll see.'

Lady Amanda moved over to the old-fashioned telephone – one of those that still had its handset actually attached to the instrument – and dialled Enid Tweedie's number (on the exceedingly old-fashioned round dial).

'Hello, Enid. Lady Amanda here. Tell me what you think of this little idea of Hugo's. He's suggested that ...'

A few minutes later, she replaced the receiver and looked at Hugo with a new respect. 'I don't know how you knew it, but it seems that you're spot on. Let's go and open up the domestic offices now, and see what sort of state they're in. I told Enid we'd have a look, and I'd ring her back if we wanted her to come up here and lend a hand.'

'But it's nearly time for dinner, Manda!'

'Yes, and in the time between now and the gong, I suggest we trot along and make use of what little time we have, and not sit here thinking about our stomachs, even if yours presents itself as a ready subject for conversation.'

'Meow!' was Hugo's only reply, and he struggled out of his chair, grabbed the walking canes he had grown accustomed to using, and began to follow her, as she left the room with one of 'those' looks on her face.

Lady Amanda had to give the door to the old kitchen a bit of a heave-ho with her shoulder before it would yield to her, and what they found revealed to them was an almost perfect Victorian kitchen, the only additions being a great deal of dust, and spiders' webs draped about the room like grey lace. In more than one nook or cranny, there was a furtive scuffling noise as the mice, the only occupants of this hithertofore deserted region of the house, made themselves scarce – race memory, coming down through several generations, warning them of the dangers of traps and cats, and especially the people who allowed these horrors to be inflicted on their species.

'Good grief, Hugo! Just look at this place!' exclaimed Lady Amanda, horrified at the condition of the kitchen. 'It looks like it belongs to Miss Havisham! We'll never get this cleaned up.'

'Don't be such a party-pooper, Manda. You can work miracles with a bit of application and an array of modern cleaning products. Remember how we changed Enid's place for her when she was in hospital? That was almost unrecognisable when we'd finished, and now she's offered to help you if you want her to. I'm sure Beauchamp will throw himself into it with enthusiasm too, if you ask him nicely.'

'I do not ask, Hugo: I command.'

'Well command nicely, then. No one likes a bossy-boots,' Hugo reminded her.

'Do you really think this midden will clean up?'

'Of course it will. It just needs time and elbow-grease. Show a bit of enthusiasm for what could be the jewel in the crown of your house tours.'

'I'll just call Beau … Argh!'

'Here, my lady,' said a voice just behind her right shoulder.

'Beauchamp! Don't do that! How can you sneak up on people without them having any idea you're there?' Lady Amanda asked him, her right hand clutched to her left breast, as she recovered from the shock. 'By nature, you're more of a Golightly than I am.'

'I've always been very light on my feet, my lady,' he explained, walking in his usual dignified manner to a space between the two of them. 'How may I be of service?'

'We rather wanted your opinion on whether it would be a good idea to open these old domestic offices to the public, for a guided tour.'

'I should say it needed a little light dusting first, my lady. Old kitchens, coal cellars, stables, and all sorts of sites of bygone domestic slavery are all the go, at the moment, I understand,' was Beauchamp's considered opinion.

'Domestic slavery! Domestic slavery? Is that what you consider yourself to be in, Beauchamp?' she squeaked in indignation.

'Heaven forbid that such a thing should cross my mind. I was, of course, referring to times gone by. And, should you be considering such a venture, may I suggest that the scullery, butler's pantry, the flower room, the boot room, and quite a number of other domestic offices might also prove useful additions to this projected tour of yours.'

'Dashed good idea, Beauchamp! Lead on! Frankly, I've no idea where to locate any of the places you just mentioned, but I'd love to have a little peek.'

Beauchamp led the way, charging stuck doors and pulling down curtains of cobwebs as he went, and the investigation of the domestic quarters was not abandoned until Lady Amanda caught something out of the corner of her eye, turned her head, and espied a large and hairy spider on her shoulder. 'Argh! Aargh! Aaargh! Get it off me! Get it off me! Oh, God, I'm going to faint!' she cried, while trying to run away from it, without thinking that it was firmly lodged on her shoulder and would not move without some help.

Hugo proved his lack of mettle by running into the recently opened pantry and shutting the door behind him, from which hiding place he shouted, 'For God's sake *do* something, somebody. I'm not coming out of here until it's gone.'

It was, of course, Beauchamp, who grabbed the offending arachnid in the soft cotton of his handkerchief, and shooed it out through a window. 'Maybe you might like to delay your return here until I have done a little light cleaning and dusting, my lady,' he suggested, with a very superior expression. 'I'm sure there are many other unwelcome visitors to these quarters, which you would be very unhappy to have to meet. I'll let you know when it is fit for you to get to work on it.

'And may I suggest, now, that you return to the drawing room where I have left a further cocktail to uphold you in your time of shock, and will sound the dinner gong in approximately fifteen minutes.' In these few sentences, Beauchamp went up even further in Lady Amanda's opinion, for not only had he been her saviour, but was willing to rid that part of the house of any other invading horrors before she had to go back for another look.

Back in the drawing room, cocktails awaiting them on the usual silver tray, Hugo took a gulp of his and announced, 'I say, Manda old bean, that was rather hairy, wasn't it?'

'So was that dratted spider,' she replied, draining her glass in one; something that had become a bit of a habit, of late. 'My goodness! That frightened the life out of me. And to think, things like that have been living in there for years. It's about time it was all rooted out and cleaned up. I'll give Enid a ring after we've eaten.'

Lady Amanda was so taken up with Hugo's plans that she had completely forgotten about the possibility that her mother might leave, and was, therefore, surprised when she came down in the morning to find the hall filled with suitcases and trunks, her mother sitting on the top of one of the latter and looking at her watch.

'You off then, Mummy? So soon? And what's all that stuff you've got in your luggage? You certainly didn't arrive with much.'

'Just a few bits and pieces I couldn't take before, given the circumstances of my departure,' replied Lady Edith, haughtily. 'I could hardly take more than a fraction of my possessions when I had to run away as I did, could I?'

'Well, as long as you haven't half-inched anything of mine,' replied her daughter.

'I have taken what was mine when I lived here. If that should include anything you thought you had subsequently inherited, you will just have to wait until I'm decently dead and buried again, won't you?'

'The second part of that could be arranged first, if you'll pass me a shovel,' replied Lady Amanda, but she said it under her breath, so that her mother couldn't hear her and pick her up on it. 'As long as you haven't taken anything I really like,' she concluded.

'I'm hardly likely to do that, am I, my dearest daughter. You have the most appalling taste, in my opinion, and I should be unlikely to reclaim anything of which you were fond.'

As Lady Amanda's face began to show the unmistakable signs of one of her outbursts, Beauchamp appeared, to defuse the situation, and announced that the taxi had arrived at the door, and the driver was awaiting his fare.

The parting of parent and child was so disgustingly insincere and two-faced that Hugo was lucky not to have witnessed it, and even Beauchamp had to go to have a little sit-down after witnessing it. It was, therefore, to a slightly emptier house that Hugo appeared for breakfast that morning, intrigued by the sight of Lady Amanda apparently dancing a jig just inside the front door, and carolling, 'Ding dong! The wicked witch is gone.'

Then, like a machine which has suddenly been switched off, she paused in mid-jig, her face became a mask of horror, and she rushed up the stairs yelling, 'The ear trumpet! The ear-trumpet! She mustn't have taken that! Oh God, please don't let her have taken the ear trumpet!'

Three minutes later, she descended the staircase at a more ladylike pace, cradling the silver ear trumpet in her arms and gazing at it fondly.

'Was all that fuss about an old ear trumpet?' asked Hugo, perplexed as to her motives for this sudden attachment to an inanimate and not very interesting object.

'Do you know how much these things are worth these days, Hugo?' she asked, looking at him in a pained manner.

'Not a clue. Going to enlighten me, then?'

'In the right auction, the best part of two grand, given the company that produced this one. And it's mine! All mine! And I intend for it to stay that way!'

Chapter Five
Actually Getting Right Down to It

Up in the attics the next morning, Lady Amanda, attempting to bounce on a mattress on one of the long-departed servants' beds, winced as she predicted a bad case of bruised buttocks.

'Surely they didn't sleep on these things?' she enquired of Hugo.

'Have you really never been up here before?' Hugo asked her, looking scandalised. 'Mind your h ...' But he was too late. Lady Amanda had risen without due care and attention, had not remembered that the bed was tucked into the eaves, and was now rubbing the top of her head, her face crumpled in pain. That's heads and tails for me, and it's only nine fifteen! she thought. Who would have thoughts that servants in this house had such daily dangers to face as giant spiders, mice, rock-hard mattresses and low-flying ceilings?

'I really don't think I'd have liked to have been in service,' she declared, moving to a part of the room that was tall enough for her to stand up properly.

'I don't think anyone would have employed you,' was Hugo's retort.

'Why ever not? I'm strong and hard-working!'

'When it suits you. You wouldn't have survived the daily grind for more than a week. No, make that more than a day,' Hugo added, as Lady Amanda did an unrehearsed little dance routine to avoid some sort of insect or another that had scuttled across the floor.

'I fear you're right, Hugo, but it doesn't mean I can't

exploit the past for the profits of the future. Now *that* I will be good at.'

'I don't doubt it, but, as I said before, you'd have been an absolutely useless servant. You'd've been forever swooning and having to have your corsets loosened.'

There's no answer to that!

Enid turned up just before lunchtime (quelle surprise!) and graciously accepted Lady Amanda's offer of joining them for a bite. Fortunately Beauchamp usually listened in on all telephone conversations, because his mistress could be a little forgetful at times, and it helped if he had the information with which to prod her memory. He had, therefore, prepared sufficient lunch for three people, and let Lady Amanda suppose that he had forgotten that Lady Edith had already left them.

After coffee, Enid was given a guided tour of the servants' quarters, and expressed shock, not only at how much there was to do, but also at the conditions they had lived in, which was outrageously outspoken for such a timid character.

'Never mind all that weeping and wailing and gnashing of teeth about things that are in the past and can't be changed. Do you think it could be done?' asked Lady Amanda, her foot tapping impatiently, while she waited for Enid to consider this.

'If I called in the Mothers' Union,' she eventually replied. 'They'd be glad to help out, to get some insight into how people used to live without it having to be on the telly. Why don't you see if they'd let you be an honorary member, Lady Amanda?'

'I'd rather eat my mother,' was her terse reply.

'Did you never want any children of your own?' asked Enid, puzzled that anyone could survive without the martyrdom of motherhood.

'Now listen to this, Enid, and listen good. When you die, they put you in a box and bury you, don't they? No, no, no! This isn't about cremation or burial. But am I right? Yes? Good! Now, as far as I'm concerned, when you have children, *they* put you in a box, and you bury *yourself*. Me? I want a life, and an unencumbered one, at that. I'm too selfish for a family, and I'm honest enough to declare it.'

'You don't mean that,' declared Enid emphatically.

'Of course she does,' Hugo gave as his opinion, but with a smile on his face.

'If they'd be happy to muck in, though, I'd be very grateful,' accepted Lady Amanda, in as humble a manner as she could muster up at such short notice, and with the thought of volunteer (free) labour, she could muster up quite a lot of humble.

'We've got our monthly meeting on Friday, and I'll put it to them then. I'm sure they'd love to have a look inside this place. They're always asking me about it,' Enid confirmed with the smug smile of one who is sought out as the fount of all knowledge on Belchester Towers.

On Monday morning, the ladies of the Mothers' Union turned up in their best pinnies, scarves tied around their heads to protect their hair-dos from dust, all of them seeming full of vim and vigour. Lady Amanda was as pleased as punch as she surveyed the eager (and nosy) faces that turned to her as she greeted them. If they were full of vim and vigour, she had just the right cleaning products for them: Vim and (from France) Vigor, a very effective spray liquid cleaner.

She was holding a clipboard as she stood before them in the hall, with all the jobs neatly parcelled out into lots. Having explained the rooms she would like 'bottomed', as Enid referred to the thorough cleansing of a room, she handed the clipboard to Enid, chirped, 'You're in charge,' and made to walk back down the hall.

'Where are you going, Lady Amanda? I thought you

were going to lend a hand and supervise; not me,' Enid called after her, her face falling. She had rather been looking forward to showing off to her friends in the MU just how friendly she and Lady Amanda were.

'Too much to do, Enid, my dear. Got to get the Christmas decorations down from the loft, hang the darned things, get the trees sorted out, write the cards, write the invitations for this Boxing Day fling – you won't mind helping out as a waitress, will you?'

'Of course not, it's just that I thought you were going to be working with us.'

'Don't be silly, Enid. I've got much more important things to do,' this called over her shoulder dismissively, as she once more disappeared into the bowels of the house in search of Beauchamp. She'd need him to help with all the boxes and things to be retrieved from the attics. And all the dashing about from floor to floor. After all, why keep a dog and bark yourself?

Hugo was waiting for her on the first floor by the lift, Beauchamp on the second floor landing by the door that led to the attics. Standing half-way between them on the second flight of stairs, she addressed her troops.

'Right! Today is "Operation Christmas Decorations". I shall retrieve them from the attics, as I know exactly where they are all kept. I shall bring them to Beauchamp,' here she nodded at the manservant, like a dowager acknowledging a peasant, 'Beauchamp will take them down to you, Hugo,' (again, the regal nod), 'and Hugo, you will load them into the lift.

'Give us a yell when it's full, and send it downstairs, so that Beauchamp can trot down and unload it, then send it back up to you. It should only take three or four trips, and we shall be done.'

'Three or four lifts' worth? Exactly how many rooms do you decorate at Christmas, Manda?' Hugo called up to her, a look of alarm on his face, at all the work to come.

Finger on forehead to promote thinking, Lady Amanda intoned, 'The drawing room, the dining room, the morning room, the library, the study, the snug, the hall …'

'OK, Manda. I get the idea. It's lucky you thought to get them down today. It'll take until Christmas Eve to get that lot done.'

'Nonsense, Hugo. We've got our little entertainment to sort out, invitations to send out, cards to write, and food and present shopping to do yet, so you'd better stop wasting time asking silly questions, so that we can get started.' And she whizzed up the final half-flight of stairs and disappeared through the door that led to the attics.

Only half an hour later, she had left the door to the steps to the attic open, and was sitting on the bottom step puffing and blowing like a grampus. Between gasps for air, she complained to Beauchamp, 'I seem to have aged ten years since we did this last year. I don't know where all my energy's gone.'

'May I suggest that my lady has had a rather busy time of it, this year, and that events have somewhat sapped her normal energy levels,' offered Beauchamp, sympathetically.

'Somewhat pompously put, but I do believe you're right. We have had some rather taxing and exciting times.'

'What's going on up there? I've been waiting ages for the next lot,' echoed up the stairwell from the floor below.

Beauchamp took over, knowing that he would have to rearrange things for the sake of efficiency and Lady Amanda's health, and called down, 'We're all going to go downstairs now, and I'll sort out a different team, using a couple of women from the Mothers' Union. We should have it done in no time, and I know you've got lists, and lists of things, to make.

'You've got the invitation list to work out, and you'll have to do a route for the tour, a script for the guide, and menus for those who are staying to tea. That should take at least this afternoon, and be sufficient work for both of you.'

'Beauchamp to the rescue as usual,' puffed Lady Amanda, struggling to rise to her feet. As she clumped heavily down the stairs to meet up with Hugo, a ghostly echo floated down behind her.

'That's Beecham!'

Hugo was more than willing to swap activities, especially since Beauchamp's suggestion involved quite a lot of sitting down. He definitely felt up to that, but he was fed up and aching from moving boxes into the lift and stacking them.

The whole exercise was playing merry hell with his back and joints – one knee in particular was giving him problems – and he knew he would enjoy sitting around planning things, which would go much easier with his arthritis.

With the two of them back in the drawing room again, Lady Amanda got herself a notepad and pencil (so that she could excommunicate with an eraser, any guest she changed her mind about) and they put their minds to those of sufficient social status to be honoured with an invitation to this exclusive gathering.

'You go first, Hugo. You've lived away a good long time, so we'll start with anyone you might like to see again – provided they're still alive, that is,' she offered, knowing that it would be her who had the final say, but she might as well let Hugo feel that he was having it as much his way, as she was, hers.

'What about Bonkers and Fluffy?' he asked, after a few moments of thought.

'Nice one, Hugo! They're connected all over the place. Just the sort of people we want to talk about our new little venture,' and she wrote on her notepad: *Colonel Henry and Mrs Hilda Heyhoe-Caramac*. 'Now, whom shall we have next?'

'Umm. Er. Got it! Blimp and Fifi. They were always good for a laugh.'

'Bulls-eye for the second time. You're good at this,' and she wrote again: *Sir Jolyon and Lady Felicity ffolliat DeWinter.* 'My turn now, I think. What about Monty and Maddie?'

'It would be good to see them again. I haven't seen them for, oh, must be thirty years, now,' Hugo agreed with alacrity, and Lady Amanda's pen moved again, as she wrote: *Major Montgomery and Mrs Madeleine Mapperley-Minto.* 'You can have another go, now, Hugo, old stick.'

Hugo scratched at his forehead, wracking his brains to come up with another name from his past. Finally he looked up and said, 'Popeye and Porky. Not long married when I lost touch with them, as I remember. Rather good to see how that worked out. They any good?'

'I'd say. I didn't even know you knew them. Although there are all those rumours about a book ... No, forget I said that.'

'Met them last time I visited the area, at old Stinky's, but that was an age ago.'

'I'll put them down. I don't know that I trust him very much, but she's all right, and their presence ought to cause a bit of a stir – not the most popular of guests in the area.' Again, she wrote: *Captain Leslie and Mrs Lesley Barrington-Blyss.*

'Why's that?' asked Hugo, curious.

'No idea,' she lied, having listened to all the gossip she found available to her, 'but I mean to find out, and Boxing Day will give us the ideal opportunity, won't it? And, as you mentioned him, what about old Stinky and Donkey?'

'Oh, yes. Hilarious couple! Had a grand time when I last went to theirs, although, as I said, it was a long time ago.'

'They haven't changed, Hugo: only got a bit older, like

we all have,' Lady Amanda assured him, turning once more to her list and noting down: *Lt Col. Aloysius and Mrs Angelica Featherstonehaugh-Armitage.* 'Now, one last couple, and I think a dozen's enough, don't you?'

'Ra-ther!' agreed Hugo.

Both of them had been lapsing into a state of deep thought between suggestions, but finally, that splendid chap, Mr Cholmondley-Crichton-Crump, opened his eyes wide, as if he had had what one used to think of as 'a light-bulb turning on' moment but, now, could no longer be pertinent to describe such an occurrence, what with the time it took to get any light brighter than a glow-worm's, for what seemed like ages, out of one those new-fangled energy-efficient jobbies.

'There's always Cutie and Daisy,' he piped up, remembering this august personage and his rather child-like and over-feminine wife, of whom he had always been rather in awe.

'Bingo!' she shouted in triumph, adding the final names to her pad: *Sir Montacute and Lady Margaret Fotherington-Flint.* 'We've done it, and in record time. I thought it would take hours to sort out a dozen people, and here we are, done in not much longer than twenty minutes. Right, I'll just leave this list, with the draft invitation I've already prepared – it's in my desk – and put it on the salver in the hall.'

'Phew! What a list! I hope the printer's got some really wide invitation cards. I'm just glad I don't have to send you one, Hugo, especially if I'd have to include all your other middle names. Anyway, Beauchamp will know what it's all about, and take it to the printer's. If I put a separate note about Christmas cards, he'll get them to print the same as usual.'

'You get your Christmas cards *printed*?' asked Hugo, aghast.

'You funny old thing! Doesn't everybody? Saves so

much time having to write them by hand, and the local printer's even got a facsimile of my signature, so that all I have to do is put them in the envelopes. He even prints the sticky labels for the envelopes. Costs a bit more than buying them in Smith's or somewhere like that, but it's worth the money to avoid the annual grind.'

'I like writing Christmas cards.'

'Well, nobody's stopping you, but you'd better get on with it, or they'll have to be New Year cards instead. Do you want me to put a PS on my note to Beauchamp to pick some up while he's in Belchester?'

'Please, Manda. I seem to have lost track of the date – not an uncommon occurrence – but a dashed nuisance if it happens when one is writing a cheque. I sent one out the other week, and it was returned to me because I'd dated it for some time in 1955.'

'Hugo! You old duffer!'

At this point a mobile pile of dust, grime and cobwebs entered the room, coughed, more from necessity than manners, and Enid Tweedie's voice issued forth from it. 'Mr Bowchamp asked us if we'd like to have a bite of lunch, to save us going home and having to come back again. He said that if it was all right with you, to tell you that your lunch would be slightly delayed, but that he was sure you wouldn't mind,' and she said this all in one breath, in case Lady Amanda would think it impertinent of her to presume that she and her crew of stout mothers might presume to eat here, as well as have the privilege of cleaning decades of dirt from its back-stairs regions.

'Absolutely no problem, dear Enid.' Lady Amanda beamed at the mobile midden, so pleased was she with the completion of the guest list, which she had considered would be a much more onerous task than it had proved, and good old Hugo had been worth his weight in gold, with the suggestions he had made.

'Hugo and I were just going to plan where to put all the

Christmas trees, weren't we, Hugo?'

'All?' queried Hugo, an expression of horror taking possession of his features.

Chapter Six
Right in the Thick of it

'Just how many Christmas trees do you put up every year?' asked Hugo, through a mouthful of cod in parsley sauce. 'We only ever had one really big one in the entrance hall. Drapings of holly, ivy, and mistletoe sufficed for all the other rooms of the house. Of course, the staff had a small one in their sitting room, but we didn't go mad. One was enough for us.'

'Well, it's never been enough for this family. Let me see ...' and she counted silently on her fingers, 'I think it's ten.'

'TEN?'

'And why not? We always liked Christmas to colour every room we used over the yuletide season, and I've seen no good reason to meddle with tradition.'

'*Where?*'

'Entrance hall, drawing room, dining room, breakfast room, study, snug, library, ballroom, morning room and first floor landing, so that the lights shine down on one, out of the darkness. So jolly! Oh, and I nearly forgot – two outside, each side of the entrance, to brighten up leaving or entering the house. And I suspect Beauchamp has at least one, in his own quarters.'

'And all this just for you?' Hugo was astounded.

'I'm worth it, aren't I? And anyway, it makes up for not being surrounded by a large and loving family at that particular time of year, which seems to be tailored for that sort of thing,' she replied, somewhat belligerently.

'But you'd hate that, wouldn't you? Scores of relatives

everywhere, running hither and thither, and generally messing up your routines.'

'Of course I would, Hugo, but it'll be an awful lot nicer, having you here, this year.'

This compliment caused Hugo to blush rather, and he looked down at his plate, studying the remaining new potatoes and peas thereon with unwarranted interest.

'Jolly decent of you to say so, old thing.'

'Not at all! Now, eat up, and we'll have our coffee and half an hour to digest, then we'll get going on those trees.'

'Were they up in the loft, too?' asked Hugo, innocently.

This question caused Lady Amanda to burst out laughing. 'You don't think I'd allow an artificial tree house room, do you? No, these were delivered to the stable-yard yesterday afternoon when you were taking your nap, and Beauchamp is going to drag them round to the front door when he's cleared away luncheon. Then we can get on with the fun bit!'

Hugo, who couldn't see where the fun was, trying to hang things on branches that were always just out of reach, and getting oneself covered in spiky needles and, occasionally, resin, the stickiest substance known to man, volunteered for an alternative duty. 'Couldn't I work on the menus for Boxing Day afternoon, instead?'

'No, you certainly cannot! That is something that I'm particularly looking forward to myself, and I don't see why you should have all the fun of that, while I'm doing something else. Besides, you're taller than me, and can reach the higher branches easier.'

'Now, how did I know that that was exactly what you were going to say?' asked Hugo, accepting the inevitable with bad grace, and producing a sulky pout that lasted until Lady Amanda passed her compact mirror over to him, and showed him his face.

Hugo hadn't realised just how big the trees that Lady

Amanda had ordered would be, and was horrified to find that most of them were about ten to twelve feet tall, with just two of them being the rather more manageable height of eight feet. When he'd gone outside to take a look, Beauchamp was lugging round a variety of containers in which to plant them, a look of resignation on his face.

As he passed Hugo, he muttered confidentially, 'I don't mind so much getting them inside and in their pots, because you do get the look of them when they're decorated to enjoy, but lugging them out again in New Year is a thankless task, and I absolutely dread it – all those pine needles everywhere, and it doesn't matter how much you clean – they keep turning up till after Easter.'

This cheered Hugo up no end, to realise that he was not the only one in the household that wasn't a hundred per cent enamoured of these seasonal decorations and, having seen the look on Beauchamp's face as he made this confession, decided to throw himself into the activity with all the enthusiasm and energy he could muster, to support the man who had to do what he was told.

It was after Beauchamp had lugged the eight giant trees into the house, only leaving the two relatively shorter ones outside, that Hugo decided to begin his good deed, and bent over to grab hold of the base of the trunk of one of them. That was his first and only mistake. With what he thought must have been an audible 'ping', his back went, and he was stuck fast, bent over the length of evergreen, unable to stand up again.

'Manda!' he cried, all the blood rushing to his head. 'Help! I'm stuck! Help, Manda! Help me!'

Lady Amanda came scooting out of the house and was brought up short by the sight of Hugo, bent nearly double, and shouting his head off. 'Whatever's the matter with you?' she asked.

'Back's gone!' he explained, using as few words as he was able, to retain his puff. 'Can't get up! Can't move!'

'Hang on there a moment, and I'll get you inside,' she instructed him.

'But I can't move!' he reiterated, before noticing that she had disappeared in the direction of the stables, returning a few moments later pushing a stout wheelbarrow.

'Lady Amanda to the rescue,' she trilled at him. 'Just stand there, and go with the flow. Don't resist anything,' she commanded.

'I can't even stand up, let alone resist any … whooo!'

Hugo yelled, as the wheelbarrow hit him square behind the knees, and he fell backwards into the old wooden contraption which Lady Amanda had thoughtfully filled with straw, before felling Hugo like a small tree with it.

'That hurt!' he spluttered in indignation, lying on his back looking up at her.

'Serves you right!' she replied, unsympathetically. 'Silly old fool, trying to drag that thing indoors. It might not be very heavy, but you know you're not supple enough to do it. I'll have to get Beauchamp to give you a good rub with horse liniment. That ought to do the job!'

At that moment, Enid slipped through the front door for a few minutes away from the dust-filled air of the domestic quarters and, looking with amusement at Hugo, overturned like a stranded tortoise in the wheelbarrow, ,commented, 'He's not the first prize in the Christmas draw, is he?' before dissolving into giggles.

Lady Amanda explained what a pickle he'd got himself into, and Enid responded immediately. 'One of our retired ladies used to work as a chiropractor. Shall I ask her to get cleaned up and come and have a look at him?'

'If you would, Enid, we'd both be most grateful,' agreed Lady Amanda. Hugo tried to smile but found that hurt too, so just lay there, like the prize pig in a rural raffle, while Enid disappeared into the house again, calling, 'Mrs Hardacre? Mrs Hardacre? Where are you?

Someone has need of your special talents,' while Lady A wandered a short distance away, where she could have a little snort of amusement without hurting Hugo's feelings.

Not only did Mrs Hardacre work wonders on Hugo's locked back, but the ladies of the Mothers' Union returned on Tuesday, to carry on their cleaning work in the attic bedrooms, and again on Wednesday, to help decorate the trees for Lady Amanda and Hugo, whom they viewed as an elderly couple in need of practical help.

By this time, Hugo, with two more treatments from Mrs Hardacre, was more sprightly than he had been before his unfortunate mishap with the tree, and Lady Amanda was busy sliding cards into envelopes, hot from the local printing press, and invitations (marked prominently RSVP ASAP) into rather grander envelopes, for their Boxing Day 'do'.

The sooner she knew how many were coming, the sooner she would be able to sort out the catering, and if they all did answer promptly, then any refusals could be filled with substitutes, with still time to RSVP before the shops closed for the festive season, and she was champing at the bit to get on with things.

Having deposited her tottering piles of envelopes on the hall table for Beauchamp to put in the post box, she sought out Hugo so that they could run through the route of the tour, and discuss any food phobias from which their guests might suffer.

She found him stretched out on a chaise longue in front of the fire, in the library, and his face was wreathed in smiles when he saw her approach. ''Lo there, Manda. Come for a li'l chitty-chatty?' he asked, his forehead creased in puzzlement at the indistinct diction he had just demonstrated.

'Are you all right, Hugo?' she asked in concern.

'Think so. Not abs'l'y sure, acksherlly,' he replied, and

Amanda went to the other side of him, to see if there was any obvious evidence of what was wrong with him. She hoped to God he hadn't had a stroke. How he (or she) would cope with that, on top of his other medical problems, she didn't dare even to think.

Her fears proved unfounded, however, as she espied at the head of the chaise longue a brandy bottle and balloon, and a box of coproxamol. The silly old bear had just about knocked himself out with strong painkillers and alcohol. 'Have you been drinking, Hugo?' she asked him acidly.

'Just a li'l one. 's only medic-ic-imal!' he stated, with inebriated dignity.

'Just a little half a bottle!' she declared, her voice rising with each word. And how many of these pills did you take?'

'Wha' pills? Don' know nothin' 'bou' no pills,' he stated, ending on a high-pitched fortissimo hiccough.

'BEAUCHAargh!' she shouted, leaping to one side, as the man seemed to emerge from the very floor.

'Yes, my lady?' asked Beauchamp, his usually bland expression somewhat challenged at the sight of Hugo with his thatch of white hair sticking up all over the place, and the idiot smile on his face.

'Mr Hugo is rather tired and emotional, Beauchamp,' Lady A stated, recovering her dignity with amazing alacrity. 'I wonder if you could see him to his room, and make sure he gets to bed without mishap.'

'As you wish, my lady,' agreed Beauchamp, and added quietly, as he turned to his task, 'I'll just get the wheelbarrow, shall I?'

'What was that? I couldn't quite catch it?' asked Lady Amanda, and couldn't understand why Hugo had just started to laugh hysterically.

'Nothing, my lady. Just encouraging Mr Hugo.'

The next day, after Hugo had refused a fried breakfast, and

settled instead for some dry toast and black coffee, Lady Amanda suggested that they get on with the menu for the dry run on Boxing Day.

'Manda! Have a heart!' Hugo exclaimed in as loud a whisper as he could. 'I'm not feeling quite the ticket. Must have been something I ate yesterday, although I've no idea what, as we ate exactly the same things.'

'I don't think eating was the problem, Hugo. Tell me, what do you remember of going to bed last night?'

Hugo sat and thought for a while, even though thinking increased the thumping headache he was nursing. 'I don't have any clear memory of going to bed, actually,' he replied, looking a mite puzzled.

'What is your last clear memory?' Lady Amanda was going to let him have the unvarnished truth about the matter, because she didn't want a recurrence, not only over the festive season, but ever.

'I was in the library,' Hugo articulated slowly, a frown creasing his brow. 'I had made the decision to have a tot of brandy, then try a little nap; just to refresh myself, you understand. Then ... well, not a lot.'

'I'm not surprised. You got yourself into a right old state, taking your painkillers and brandy – about half a bottle, I estimated, and BeauchaARGH! I wasn't actually calling you: I was just mentioning your name. Now run along and get back to whatever it was you were doing. I really must get you some shoes with steel heel and toe-caps, or bells on them, or something, anything just to warn me of your arrival.'

The manservant left the room, smiling mischievously to himself and stifling a chuckle, as Lady Amanda continued, 'Now, where was I? Oh, yes, you were in fact sozzled! As squiffy as a drunken sailor! As pissed as a newt – if you'll excuse the vernacular. You were, in fact, steaming drunk, Hugo, and Beauchamp,' (she whispered his name this time), 'had to fetch the wheelbarrow and put you to bed to sleep it off.'

'No!' exclaimed Hugo, accidentally raising his voice in surprise, then wishing he hadn't, as all the little men with mattocks started digging away at the bedrock of his brain again.

'Yes, Hugo, and it just won't do. A cocktail or three – fine, no problem. A bucket of spirits, however, is too reminiscent of Grandpapa, who couldn't face the day without a snifter of brandy first thing in the morning.'

'I never knew he was a tippler,' said Hugo with a grimace of effort, as he tried to place Lady A's grandpapa.

'More of a toper, although it was hardly noticeable until he had to write anything, then all he could do was a sort of scribble, because he was too far gone for his coordination to work efficiently. He was known by his contemporaries as Old Scribbler, which is just as well, for in his later years, he was more like Old Dribbler.

'Now, have you taken anything for that birdcage mouth, the little men drilling in your head and the stomach like a stormy sea?'

'No,' he replied, groaning as she reminded him of his individual symptoms, 'And it's not drills, it's mattocks: little men with mattocks,' he informed her for the sake of accuracy.

'What an old-fashioned hangover you're having. And as for the way you're feeling, I'll get Beauchamp to make you one of his prairie oysters – goes down like fire, but cleanses as it goes, and leaves you feeling as right as ninepence.'

'Who's old-fashioned now? That should surely be as right as 4p. Urhhh!'

On queue with the groan, Beauchamp stepped smartly into the room with a tall glass on a small silver salver. 'For you, Mr Hugo,' he intoned, leaning forward to offer the glass. 'I noticed how you looked this morning, and thought you would probably feel a lot more human after one of these.'

Hugo eyed the glass, and it eyed him back. With a start, he asked, 'How can I drink that when it's looking at me?'

'That's only the egg yolk, sir. It'll slip down without you even noticing.'

'And no doubt reappear within a few seconds looking for an encore.' Hugo was very dubious about the contents of the glass.

'Trust me, sir. I have been ministering to hangovers in this house since I was a boy, and I haven't lost a patient yet.'

'Hold your nose while you drink it, Hugo, old bean. It'll make it easier to swallow if you can't taste it.'

With two pairs of eyes scrutinizing him closely as to what he would do next, Hugo pinched his nostrils together with the forefinger and thumb of his left hand, while lifting the glass to his lips, and tossing off the contents almost in one swallow.

He sat in silence for a while, colour slowly returning to his cheeks, then he opened his mouth and made a sound like an air-raid siren. After this sound had ceased, he sat back in his chair, ran a hand through his thatch of white hair, and smiled. 'I don't know what you put in that, Beauchamp, but it seems to have worked a miracle. What was it?'

Lady Amanda butted in as he finished speaking. 'You really don't want to know Hugo. Just be grateful that you got it down, and it's staying down. I can see you look better already. Which is good, because today I wanted to go over the menu with you for our experimental opening of the house. I suggest, however, that, given the delicate state of your constitution, we do nothing until after lunch.'

'Good-oh! I might feel human again, but I think I'll just go to my room and have a little lie-down. I didn't sleep soundly last night, as I was haunted by the most peculiar dreams. After Beauchamp's contribution to my constitution, however, I feel I shall sleep like the dead. Perhaps you would be so good as to wake me just before the gong for luncheon.' And with that, he rose from his place at the table, folded his napkin, and made as hasty a retreat as he could manage from the room.

'Thank you for your anticipation, Beauchamp. That will be all for now,' Lady A trilled at her manservant, and was unaware of the muttered 'Beecham' from him, as he headed back to his own corner of the house.

Chapter Seven
Reactions and Counter-Reactions

Through letterboxes all over the county were dropping thick white envelopes, containing social dynamite. The postman was delivering the invitations that Lady Amanda had written and caused to be posted the day before.

In the Heyhoe-Caramac residence, it was the housekeeper who delivered the mail to Colonel Henry and Mrs Hilda, when breakfast had been cleared away. Both master and mistress were still sitting at the dining table, enthralled in items in their separate newspapers, when the post was slapped down on the table in front of the colonel.

Without comment about the slapdash way in which their mail had been delivered, as this had become the norm over the last year or so, he picked up the pile of envelopes and went through them, commenting on each one, and making a pile for himself and a separate pile for his wife.

'Christmas card, Christmas card, Christmas card, letter from Letitia,' he began, slapping four envelopes in a pile for his wife's perusal. 'Bill – damn and blast it! Has that tailor no patience? Another bill – damned wine merchant, this time, I suppose. Why he couldn't have waited until the New Year I shall never know.' That was two in his pile, as he continued, 'Readers' Digest – no doubt we're in a draw to win £100,000.' This envelope he tossed towards the fireplace, to be consumed by the hungry flames.

'Bank statement – that's mine. Christmas card, Christmas card, Christmas card – all for you, I presume, my dear. Hello! What's this?' he concluded, holding up the velvety envelope in which their invitation from Lady

Amanda was enclosed. 'Don't recognise the handwriting, so we'll both take a look at that. Three more Christmas cards, and that's it for today. Shall we have a look inside our mystery envelope first, Fluffy?'

'Please, Bonkers. I'm dying to know what it is. Maybe one of our friends is having a New Year's Ball, and we're to be invited,' gushed his wife, always one to live in hope.

Colonel Henry – aka Bonkers – used his thick thumb as a rather inefficient letter-opener, and pulled out the stiff oblong of card from within its folds. His wife Hilda – aka Fluffy – looked on with the face of someone who always sees their glass as half-full rather than half-empty, and chided him to hurry up, as his eyes widened, his nostrils flared, and his mouth fell open. 'Well, what is it, Bonkers? Come on: hurry up and stop teasing me. It's an invitation, isn't it? From whom? To what? When?'

'Damn and blast the woman!' exclaimed her husband, holding the oblong of cream card at arm's length, the better to focus on it. 'Trust her to make us an invitation we couldn't refuse; although we could fake illness, or even death, if we wanted to.'

'What are you babbling about, Bonkers? What woman? Invitation to what? Why can't we refuse? Why should we need to fake illness or death?' This morning was proving to be full of unanswered questions for poor old Fluffy Heyhoe-Caramac, and she could feel her kipper turning sour in her stomach with the upset of it all.

'It's that ghastly Golightly female – dreadful woman …'

'I rather like her,' interrupted his wife, only to find herself uncharacteristically slapped down for her comment.

'Shut up, woman, and listen to this.'

'There's no need to be so rude about it. Whatever it is, it's not my fault.'

'Sorry, Fluffy. Just got my dander up, that's all. She

wants us to go to that fearful fake castle of hers on Boxing Day?'

'What for? What use could we be to her on Boxing Day?'

'There's some blether here about her opening the house for guided tours – stuff and nonsense, if you ask me – and she wants to do a trial run with some of her friends – ha ha! Good one, that! – with afternoon tea thrown in, to see if: a) we would give her some feedback on the quality of the tour and food, and: b) to see if we would recommend it to any of our friends – people of the right background who wouldn't pinch the silver or spill things on the furnishings.'

'Does she actually say that?' asked Fluffy, now fascinated with what she was being told. 'In those exact words?'

'No, silly, she just implies it. I'm perfectly able to read between the lines, and if there's a sub-text to anything, you know I'll find it. She seems to be attempting to break into the lucrative tourist market, using us as guinea-pigs and free advertising.'

'Do we have to pay for the tour and the tea?' asked Fluffy in a more practical vein than her husband.

'No: it's to be free for trial, to a few select friends.'

'Then we'll go,' stated Fluffy, decisively. 'You know how annoyed you always get on Boxing Day, when all the poor relations and local scroungers show up, hoping to be shown a bit of seasonal largesse. Then you get a terrible gastric attack because you're so infuriated, and I hardly see you again till New Year.

'This year we'll be out when they arrive, and they can stay on the doorstep for as much of the day as they care to. We shall be elsewhere, getting a free feed for once, and your digestive system will, no doubt, purr like a cat in consequence. So, let's have no more of this looking a gift horse in the mouth, and accept with a good grace.'

'Do you know, you're a genius, Fluffy? You're absolutely right! Maybe Popeye and Stinky will be there too. It could prove to be a very enjoyable afternoon, being shown behind closed doors, then being waited on and fed like royalty. I'm going to write and accept this very minute. Trust you to find a completely different way of looking at things.'

'That's because I always look on the bright side, Bonkers, unlike you, who would probably have found fault with the Garden of Eden,' she informed him, only for him to score an unexpected point by adding,

'Never did like apples. Now, that would have made a very interesting story.'

She aced his serve, but only in her head by thinking that he only didn't like the woman because she was a better shot than him, and his pride was wounded more often than the game, when he was shooting.

At The Manor, Sir Jolyon *ff*olliat DeWinter – aka Blimp – sniffed suspiciously at the thick expensive envelope that had arrived with that morning's post, wrinkled his nose, and handed the missive to his wife Lady Felicity, with a sound that may only be represented in the written form as 'Hrmph!'

'What's that you're passing to me?' asked Lady Felicity – aka Fifi – suspiciously. Anything not addressed solely to her, that her husband passed over for her to deal with, usually spelled trouble, and the dark side of her curiosity was instantly aroused. 'What horrible nest of vipers are you handing over to me now?' she asked, taking the offered piece of correspondence, and working at it with her marmalade-smeared knife, in order to set loose the snakes.

'Whatever it is, I'm neither giving nor donating anything, taking part, buying anything, or getting involved in any way,' replied her husband, leaving the whole thing to his wife to deal with.

'Oh!' Fifi exclaimed in surprise. 'It's an invitation. Now, let me just look at the details before I tell you about it.'

'I'm not going to any auctions or fund-raising dinners,' stated her husband, his figure swelling with indignation at the very thought, and explaining why, at an early age, he had been nicknamed 'Blimp'. 'I don't want to sponsor anyone or anything, nor do I wish to attend any exhibitions of new and exciting artists, whose work will be a splendid investment for the future. I'm fed up with being rooked and preyed on, and that's all anyone ever wants these days: to dip their hand into my wallet, and leave it a little thinner than it was before they came along.'

'You'll be well-pleased to find out that it's to something that is absolutely scot free, then. It won't cost you a penny, we'll get a little look behind the scenes at a well-known local residence, and fed, into the bargain.'

'I say, Fifi. That sounds more like it. Go on.'

'It's from Lady Amanda Golightly, and invites us to Belchester Towers for a free tour of certain quarters of the property, with a slap-up afternoon tea thrown in. If we're willing to stay behind and give her some feedback on the experience, and maybe dig up a few friends of the right calibre to pay to do the tour in the spring, we can stay to cocktails as well. There! What do you think of that?'

'When is it?' asked her husband, his face beginning to clear like a grey day after rain, his smile representing the sun, which was definitely coming out from behind one of the last clouds.

'Boxing Day,' replied his wife, noting his change of mood. 'What do you think?'

'I think that's rather splendid!' replied her husband. 'I've always hated the twenty-sixth – no character whatsoever, and everyone making do with left-overs from the day before and pretending it's all a jolly jape to be eating food that should have been fed to the pigs before something completely original had been cooked instead. The hunt used to be the only highlight of a rather grim day, and that's gone for ever now, more's the pity.'

'That's a 'yes' then, is it?' Blimp never said one word when ten would do the job just as well.

'It's a splendid idea, and I should love to have a look round that old place. I haven't been there since we were courting. Do you remember that fake priest hole that the original Golightly had constructed when the building was first going up?'

'Yes, to the first question, and how on earth could you remember when the place was first built? You'd have to be over two hundred years old to be able to do that.'

'Family story. Passed down. But, I say, it was rather fun in that old priest hole, wasn't it?'

Fifi blushed, and turned her attention to her other mail. She didn't feel that the breakfast table was a fitting place to remember the follies and indiscretions of youth. 'I'll reply in the affirmative then, shall I?' she asked, opening another envelope which obviously contained a Christmas greeting from one of their friends.

'Definitely! Tally-ho! and all that. Maybe we can raise the ghost of a memory, if the tour visits a certain little cell.'

At The White House, Belchester, a rather more modest residence than the two that had already received their summons, Madeleine Mapperley-Minto usually dealt with the mail, as its contents often had the effect of upsetting her husband to the extent that he had to wander off in search of a little tot of something to soothe his nerves.

She had put this practice into place after one particularly bad week when nothing but bills had arrived, Monty's little tot had turned into a bit of a binge, and she had taken refuge in several bottles of rather bad white wine, not because they usually drank the bad stuff, but because she knew that the way she would throw it down her throat, taste would be the last of her considerations of its quality.

She was, not unnaturally, a little wary, as she knocked discreetly on the door of his study, to apprise him of the arrival of an invitation. 'There's something I need to speak to you about, Monty,' she announced in a firm voice as she entered the room holding the invitation card in her hand.

Monty's eyes fixed on it as if it were a cobra, risen and ready to strike, and she could see him swallow as he started to salivate at the thought of something that annoyed him and sent him into a rage, with the inevitable following administration of a few pegs, to calm his nerves and restore his good humour.

'Now, don't get yourself into a state. Just listen to what I have to say before you even think of going off to empty the decanters. This is a lovely invitation, and I'm sure it will put you in a good mood just hearing about it,' said Maddie, diplomatically and firmly.

'Lady Amanda Golightly has invited us to a rather unusual event which is to take place on Boxing Day and, as it mentions cocktails at the end, I thought you might be tempted to attend.'

'That's a good start. What's she up to?'

'She wants to consult a group of friends – from the right circles, of course – to try out an idea she has, of giving guided tours of certain parts of her residence. There will be afternoon tea afterwards and, for those who don't mind, as I said, staying on to give feedback and, perhaps, recommend her new enterprise to 'suitable' friends, there will be cocktails served.'

'What, no wine with the afternoon rations?' asked her husband, rather churlishly, thought Maddie.

'You know very well that you'll take your hip flask, no matter what, and you also know that I know that you hate

Christmas. At least this would get us out of the house, and she's bound to have invited other people that we know, so I think it could turn out to be rather a jolly 'do'.'

'OK, then.'

'What, no argument? No need for me to plead with you?'

'No! I've heard that she's hooked up with old Chummy – you remember Hugo Cholmondley-Crichton-Crump, don't you?'

'I could hardly forget him, with a name like that, could I?' replied Maddie, finding herself unexpectedly smiling. She had thought she faced a much harder task than this had proved to be.

'Fancy a chin-wag with old Chummy. Haven't seen him in donkey's. Thoroughly good chap!'

'That's settled then. I'll drop Lady Amanda a note of acceptance,' said Maddie, hardly believing her luck.

'Splendid!' commented her husband, and returned his attention to the *Financial Times* without a hint of going off in search of alcoholic stimuli.

Captain Leslie (Popeye) Barrington-Blyss of Journey's End, Belchester, would never leave an important task like opening the mail to his meek but solidly built wife, Lesley, whom everyone who knew her well enough addressed affectionately as 'Porky'.

Their long-term nicknames were easily explained by stating that Capt Leslie (he still insisted on his rank being used) had been careless enough to lose an eye and wore, as a consequence, a black eye-patch. Being the sort of man that he was, he wasn't beyond popping out his false eye to frighten both servants and children alike for his own crass amusement. As for Porky, she had been a well-built child who had never lost her puppy fat, later adding the extra weight she had gained by having two children quite late in life, and was now as round and bouncy as a rubber ball.

In the mail this morning, Capt Leslie had received an invitation to Lady Amanda's 'Belchester Towers Tours (with afternoon tea provided)' trial run, and had seized on this as a superb opportunity for him to do a little snooping. He was writing a book – 'County Characters – Unmasked' was its working title – and this would give him carte blanche, not only to poke around a bit in a house he had barely seen for years, but to eavesdrop on the other guests, who would probably be known to him, and thus provide grist for his literary mill.

Without consulting his wife, he penned a reply in the very worst purple prose, and walked down to the post box to send it, before Lesley could offer her opinion, and maybe try to scupper the idea of going at all.

On his return, he threw the information casually into a conversation they were having about Christmas arrangements in general, and waited for her reaction with bated breath.

To his surprise, she seemed utterly enchanted at the idea. 'What a lovely idea! It's about time a few more people got a look at that intriguing house, and you know how boring I find the twenty-sixth. I shall, of course, have to have a new frock though – I've absolutely nothing to wear.'

'That's because you keep growing out of everything in your wardrobe,' said her husband spitefully, but he said it sotto voce, so that she shouldn't hear him and cause a scene. Goodness me, the tent-makers were going to be busy between now and Christmas Day! was his last unkind thought on the matter, before he moved the conversation on to an inquisition on why the house-keeping accounts seemed to be so high over the last month, wanting every last penny accounted for to his satisfaction. This was one of his favourite pastimes, and he enjoyed himself thoroughly for the next hour and a half.

At Squire's Court, Lady Margaret (Daisy) Fotherington-Flint came rushing out of her dressing room in her lacy dressing-gown, hooting like a siren and making little squeaking noises of happiness and excitement. She headed straight for her husband, Sir Montacute (Cutie)'s dressing room, almost skipping at the pleasant news she had to impart.

Without knocking, she sailed into the room, catching Sir Montacute fighting with his socks, in an effort to be ready for breakfast on time. Looking at him wrestling to catch his feet and capture them in sober black cashmere, she thought how fitting his nickname had been all his life. From photographs, she knew he had been a pretty baby who had grown into a beautiful child, and from this state of development, into a handsome man, as he still was in his later years, and she felt a thrill of pride that she had captured him and that he was still hers.

'What the devil do you think you're doing, bursting in on me like that, without any warning whatsoever?' he asked, a little grumpily. A man should be allowed to dress in privacy, and not be interrupted when he was in the puffing and blowing acrobatic mode that this pastime now represented, now that he was not in his first, or even second, flush of youth. Dressing had become an undignified occupation that should not be viewed by anyone, least of all his wife, for whom the perfection of his daily turnout should not be marred by the exertions needed to achieve that state every day.

'Oh, Cutie, don't be cross with me. I have such exciting news. We've had an invitation to something that sounds fun, fun, fun!' An unbiased observer may have, at this point, wondered how, if this was how Daisy normally behaved, her handsome husband had put up with this sort of girlish behaviour for so many years.

'What's that?' asked her husband, now attempting to put his feet into his shoes, and having quite a time of it with his aim. 'I hope it's not another blasted charity ball. I'm not made of money, you know, and times are hard.'

'It's from Lady Amanda, and it won't cost you a penny, Cutie, my darling,' she cooed back at him, not at all ruffled by his grumpy responses. She had learnt to ignore them years ago, and they hardly registered at all on her consciousness now.

'Damned pleased to hear it! What's the old wind-bag up to now, then?'

'She's planning to do guided tours of The Towers, and she wants us to be guinea pigs.'

'Oh, God! I hope that doesn't mean being dragged from room to room while some wrinkly old worthy spouts on about their boring family history.'

'Nothing of the sort, my sweet. We're to have access to bits of her residence that we've never seen before, and then be provided with afternoon tea – a no doubt splendid affair, given that she only acts mean, and is actually rolling in it.'

'Glad to hear someone is.'

'Do be quiet, Cutie, and let me finish,' she chided him, automatically. 'If we're willing to stay on and give her our opinions, we'll be included in cocktails. She wants this thing up and running by spring, and to have exactly the right sort of clients booking the tours: personal recommendation only, for the first month or so.'

'Well, cocktails sound super. Keeping the old cupboard stocked with the hundreds of bottles that seem to be required to have even a modest cocktail party these days is simply beyond my means. And if it means that I can recommend this tour to all those acquaintances that I thoroughly dislike, that will be the icing on the cake. When's this shindig scheduled to happen?'

'Boxing Day,' replied his wife, pleased with the reaction she had received to the invitation.

'Hallelujah! There is a God after all! I can now cancel

my snivelling cousins who always take the trouble to have a good old suck at my wallet on the twenty-sixth. They can go hang, for we have a prior engagement, and cannot be here to receive them this year. I feel so happy about telling them, that I could kiss Lady Amanda's hand. I just hope she doesn't change her mind and cancel at the last minute. The County grapevine is every bit as efficient as the community variety.'

'Well, that's that settled, then. I shall write to accept, straight away.' Skipping like the child she had once been, Lady Margaret returned down the landing to her boudoir, where she sat at a tiny Davenport, extracted her pen and a sheet of paper embossed with her name and address, and began to write, in a beautifully flowing hand.

At the breakfast table in The Old Convent, Lieutenant Colonel Aloysius Featherstonehaugh-Armitage – aka Stinky – puffed on his after breakfast cigar, perusing the oblong of fine quality card that he held out in front of him, with interest.

'Golly, Stinky, no wonder that's what they called you when you were old enough to smoke those vile things. I do so wish you wouldn't smoke one at the breakfast table, though. Thoroughly bad form, if you ask me,' commented his wife, Angelica, affectionately known by her friends and family as 'Donkey', because she could be a bit slow at times, and as stubborn as her nickname-sake.

'Sorry old girl, but a man's got to be able to do what he wants in his own home, as there's nowhere else he can do it. Why don't you take breakfast in bed? That should solve everything. I could have my morning cigar, and you could have your breakfast in the unpolluted air of the bedroom. What do you say, old thing?'

'The air in there isn't exactly pure when you've spent the night in there.' (Amongst their friends and acquaintances, they were about the only two who still shared a bedroom.) 'I presume they didn't give you your nickname just because you took up smoking those dreadful things. You must have had it from a very early age. I wonder if it's time we had separate rooms, my little snuggle bunny. I know how my tossing and turning, and my snoring disturb you. Maybe you'd like to consider *that* over your breakfast cigar?'

'Sorry,' apologised Stinky. 'Went off into a brown study there. Didn't take in a thing you said.'

'Never mind. I'm sure I shall raise the subject again in the near future, maybe as a New Year's resolution.'

'Jolly good show, Donkey, old girl. Talk to me about it another time, what?'

'Of course, my dear. That invitation's given me an idea, though. Why can't we do the same thing here?'

'What same thing?' Lt Col. Featherstonehaugh-Armitage was still not paying his wife any attention. 'What invitation?'

'Oh, I do wish you'd listen sometimes. We've been invited to Belchester Towers on Boxing Day to do a trial run on a guided tour. We'll get a slap-up afternoon tea afterwards, and if we can be bothered to stay on and tell Lady Amanda what we think of her tour, we'll get cocktails as well,' she explained, speaking in a rush, because she was so fed up with repeating herself. She sometimes wondered whether her husband needed a hearing-aid or a resounding slap.

'Having people round for cocktails, you mean?' Stinky was still rather in the dark.

'No! Oh, I do wish you'd pay attention. Opening up part of this place to the public. Restore some of the nuns' cells, maybe do up the chapel a bit, and offer cream teas – at an extra cost, of course.'

'Ah, got you, Donkey. Go on a reconnaissance mission. Clever old thing. Not like you at all to have a brainwave. Are you feeling quite the ticket today?'

'Don't be so cutting, my dear. I'm not the utter ass you've always assumed I am. I just save my good ideas for really important things, and don't squander them on trivialities.'

'Good girl, good girl!' soothed Stinky, completely immersed in his newspaper. 'I say! Old Binky's getting a new ball-and-chain. Says so right here, in the forthcoming marriages section. At least no one could be more of an old misery-guts than the last one. Always moaning about being ill with something or other.'

'She *did* die, dear, so she must have been right. Don't be so hard on her memory.'

'You're right. Dear old Donkey! Always trying to bring out the best in people. Still, I suppose you've got your work cut out with me. I say, haven't you, old girl? Got your work cut out with me?'

'If you weren't such a fine-looking specimen, I should have poisoned you years ago and gone in search of pastures new,' replied Daisy but, Stinky was oblivious to his wife's words, reading the obituary of an old army comrade-in-arms.

Chapter Eight
Menus and Stockings and Lashings of Good Cheer

While the various invitations were being received and considered, Lady Amanda had encountered Hugo in rather finer fettle than he had been before his first ever encounter with one of Beauchamp's prairie oysters, and had cornered him so that she could bully him into joining her at a little menu planning for Boxing Day.

'Come on Hugo! You know you want to really! You've always loved a party, and you could pack away canapés faster than anyone I knew. I'm sure your educated stomach – and palate, of course – could come up with some wonderful ideas for our little tea party.

'It's got to be special, to get them to tuck in and prolong their stay: then we have to keep them hooked into the occasion long enough for cocktails to be served. That'll get 'em going. Relax them with a shot or two of alcohol, and the truth about what they really think of our enterprise, and this establishment, will come pouring out, and all without any guile whatsoever.'

'Then you don't consider that coercing them to stay for cocktails to loosen their tongues is in any way a use of guile?' asked Hugo, astonished at her attitude.

'Of course not. It's normal social practice, as far as I'm concerned, and the whole bang-shoot of them would agree with me, were they in a similar position. Come along, Hugo! Get your thinking cap on. Let's go and sit in the drawing room and see what we can come up with.'

A few minutes later, Lady A sat with a pad on her lap, a pen in her right hand, waiting for Hugo's first suggestion.

'Come along, old thing. I can't wait for ever.'

'You go first,' grumbled Hugo. 'My mind is a complete blank. You'll have to crank it over like we all used to with the old cars.'

'I think you need new batteries, if the truth be told, Chummy. Right, here goes: those lovely little squares of rusked bread with cream cheese and smoked salmon, with a little dollop of caviar on the top.'

'That's pushing the boat out a bit, isn't it?' asked Hugo, surprised at the extravagance of her first suggestion.

'We want to get them relaxed and content, don't we?' she parried.

'S'pose so! What about doing something similar with smoked venison and haggis, with a tiny drop of Cumberland sauce on top, finished off with just the merest hint of Scottish gravy?' Hugo said, a greedy look entering his eyes. This was one of his favourite nibbles.

'I'm sure the whisky supply will stand up to that. Now, what do you think of anchovy toast?'

'Absolutely topping, Amanda, old bean. Love the stuff. Can we use toasting forks and make our own toast at the fire, so that's it's hot and crispy, and not cold and limp, as it always is when made in the kitchen, then transferred to the table?'

'Superb idea! That will tie in with the tour of the domestic quarters, and let them remember how it had always limped to the table in a parlous state when made in advance.'

Lady Amanda had hardly had time to write down this idea before Hugo had another brilliant idea. 'And we could have some of those prune things wrapped in bacon. The chaps always gobble those down.'

'Better remember to get Beauchamp to de-stone the prunes, then,' remarked Lady A rather sharply, 'or there'll be cracked dentures all over the floor,' then added, 'We could do with some of those little puff pastry case things –

damn! I can't remember what they're called, but you can put a variety of fillings in them. Vol-au-vents o – that's the little beggars.

'They're a bit 'Tupperware party'-ish, aren't they?' asked the Educated Stomach.

'Have you ever actually been to a Tupperware party, Hugo?' asked Lady Amanda, skewering him with her eye.

'Well, no …'

'Then don't talk about things about which you know nothing.'

'I suppose you have been to one, then. Just your sort of thing, I suppose: pieces of plastic for a kitchen you never enter.' Hugo was now feeling quite waspish.

'I have actually,' replied his hostess, with a smile of triumph on her face. 'It was about twenty years ago, at Enid's house, when times were hard and she was trying to make a little extra money.'

'Bet you didn't buy anything.'

'Well, there, you're wrong. I did.' Lady A definitely had the winning hand in this game.

'What?' asked Hugo, mesmerised by the idea of Lady Amanda in Enid's tiny little house in Plague Alley, at something as mundane and common as a Tupperware party.

'Well, the demonstrator, as I think she was called, called it a Yorkshire pudding batter maker, but I think she must not have been trained very well. To my eye, it was a plastic cocktail shaker, for use in dire emergencies, and I immediately entered one on my order form. If one forgets the real thing on picnics, it could be a life-saver, when one is in the middle of the countryside, without a civilised dwelling in sight, and nothing in which to mix the cocktails.'

'By George! I didn't think they sold anything useful,' exclaimed Hugo, and gave her leave to add vol-au-vents to the menu, provided she could come up with some appropriate fillings.

After a few moments of silence in which she contemplated this challenge, she smiled, looked Hugo straight in the eye and said, 'What about a little melted Camembert, topped with a sharp fruit jus? Or chopped game, set in a port aspic, with a crunchy little morsel of green on the top?'

'Manda, I think you just made the vol-au-vent fit for civilised company. Of course, we haven't even started to discuss sandwiches or cakes yet, which are the main components of a good afternoon tea. No plates of bread and butter for us, on such an important occasion, I assume.'

'Absolutely not. I suggest rare beef with horseradish,' replied the hostess, licking her lips in anticipation.

'Thinly sliced pork with an apple and cinnamon sauce,' interjected Hugo, raising his voice just a tad against a tremendous rumble from his stomach. 'Golly, this is making me hungry, Manda. What time is Beauchamp bringing through afternoon tea?'

'Not long! Now think! It's better to think of food when you're hungry, because you have more enthusiasm for it. Smoked salmon and watercress. If there are any vegetarians, and I haven't seen any of these folk for some time, they'll just have to peel away the bread and eat that. Now for cakes. Over to you, Hugo.'

'Walnut and coffee, with a coffee butter cream filling and outside coating. Golly, I feel positively faint with hunger.'

'Double chocolate cake with a fresh whipped cream filling,' continued his partner, 'and I think a good old-fashioned seedcake for those who like a little punishment with their luxuries.'

The door opened soundlessly, and Beauchamp entered the room and slid across the floor as silently as a snake, a large laden tray in his hands. Hugo actually clapped his hands in glee. 'Oh, thank God you're here, Beauchamp. Here we've been discussing the afternoon tea for the twenty-sixth for I don't know how long, and I'm dying of starvation just thinking about all that food.'

As Beauchamp set down the tray, Lady Amanda tore a page out of her notebook and handed it to him. 'Cast your eye over that, will you, and let me know if there are any problems, or if there is anything you would like to add to the list. We must do our guests proud on this occasion, because so much depends on it.'

Beauchamp took a cursory glance at the list and, just before he took his leave of them, murmured, 'Bite-sized lemon meringue pies. Individual treacle tarts with a creme patissiere topping ...'

'Just add them to the list, my good man. I'm sure anything you come up with will be gastronomically excellent.'

The fact that the afternoon tea that had been set before them wasn't of the gourmet quality they had been discussing, made no difference whatsoever, so hungry had their menu-planning session made them, and they fell on the food with gusto, and slightly less good manners than usual.

The next few days saw the arrival of six envelopes, all containing acceptances to Lady Amanda's invitation, and by Christmas Eve, she was literally rubbing her hands together in glee at the thought of her forthcoming advertising campaign, cunningly disguised as a plea to her friends' good taste, and for their generosity in spreading the word of the future opening of the official tours.

'I don't understand why you're so excited at this commercial enterprise, Manda,' stated Hugo during the afternoon. 'I mean, it's not as if you need the money, is it?'

'Of course not! Don't be so coarse! I like people, and I

haven't seen enough of them in recent years. Running into you has brought that home to me. Not only have I gladly accepted you into my house and enjoyed your company, but I have also craved more. I thoroughly enjoyed our little adventure earlier in the year, and as something like that isn't likely to land in our laps again, I'm making the effort to be more sociable.

'I'm basically a very nosy person, and have found myself in a position to have no one to be nosy about. If I can get nothing out of this enterprise except the renewing of old friendships, it will be enough. If it actually works, I shall be meeting different people every week, and life will be more fun. Though I did like being a detective! Still, I suppose I shouldn't wish someone dead, just because I want to play at being 'Shirley' Holmes again.'

'Does that mean you don't really want *me* here?' asked Hugo, not quite understanding what she was trying to tell him, with all this talk of meeting different people every week to make life fun again.

'Exactly the opposite. After a few initial hiccoughs, I think we've settled down admirably together. And renewing our friendship has made me hungry for other contact. You've breathed new life into me, Hugo, old boy, and I shall be eternally grateful for that. Now, don't forget to hang up your stocking on the fireplace tonight, will you?'

'Whatever for?' Hugo sounded scornful. 'We're hardly children any more.'

'Let me tell you a little story, Hugo, old bean. When I first got my state pension, I put the money towards financing the best cocktail cabinet in the county. When I'd done that, I had the money paid into a special account, to which only Beauchamp has access – I trust him implicitly with my funds.

'From this, every Christmas, he buys himself anything he wants, as a gift from me. The remaining funds are to buy me presents. He is my own personal Father Christmas, and it's much more exciting than when I was a child, because he always knows exactly what I want, even if I haven't realised it yet. This year, you're on his present list, too, and as you've been a good boy all year, to my knowledge, you'd better be prepared to hang up that old stocking, and get what's coming to you, in the morning.'

'Why don't you just donate it to charity?' asked Hugo, somewhat ungratefully, she thought.

'Because I already make generous donations to charities throughout the year, and this is my one annual indulgence, to which I feel I'm entitled.'

Hugo sat for a moment, lost in thought, while he digested what she had just told him, then sat bolt upright and looked straight at her. 'You're absolutely right, my dear, as always. And may one ask if there is any limit to the size of the stocking I'm allowed to leave out?'

'A yacht is completely out of the question, but I leave the size to your own discretion. Anything that won't fit will be left by the fireplace, with your name on it.'

'I think I'm going to enjoy this Christmas. You're going to make it just as sparkling and magical as it used to be in the old days, before I got old and crippled and stopped going out. It's not a time of year to be on one's own, and I don't have children to visit or to invite me round. I thank God every time I remember old Reggie, that you were on a mission to cheer up his day, and arrived in that ghastly nursing home while I was in residence.'

They attended Midnight Mass with Beauchamp chauffeuring the Rolls. It was a custom that neither of them liked to miss, although Hugo, of later years, had had to make do with the first Eucharist of Christmas on the television. When they had been younger, it didn't matter how long the party had been going on, they all pulled themselves together to go as a large group for this special service, and managed to behave themselves during its lease.

Tonight was a bit like old times, as they remembered those Christmases of so very long ago, and the people who used to be such good friends, before the war had intervened, and they had either been killed, or been scattered all over the world. They might be old, but at least they had gay and happy memories, and, hopefully, would spend the last years of their lives enjoying each other's company, and not being alone on all the important days throughout the year.

When they arrived back at Belchester Towers after the service, even though it was twelve forty-five, they did not go directly to bed. Old people do not need so much sleep, and they repaired to the drawing room where Beauchamp brought through a tray with three cocktails on it, as he always celebrated the dawn of another Christmas as a member of the family, and not just a hired help. That was how things had always been, and they would not change in Lady Amanda's lifetime.

'Well, what have you cooked up for us this Christmas?' asked Lady Amanda, as Christmas cocktails were always Beauchamp's choice.

'I have provided a 'White Christmas' for you, my lady, as I noticed the first few flakes of snow falling as I put away the Rolls. Mr Hugo, I know, has been having problems with one of his knees, so for him, I have prepared a 'Wobbly Knee', which I thought was very appropriate. And for myself, a new recipe which rejoices in the unusual name of a 'Bumpo'. I have no idea what it means, or even what it tastes like, but I like a surprise. Cheers! Merry Christmas to you both! And to you both, a peaceful New Year!' Beauchamp had no idea how he had tempted fate with his toasts, and this was his second offence.

The next morning reminded Hugo of his childhood

Christmases. Strings of white lights had appeared, draped round every room, and every Christmas tree in the house was ablaze with lights. Holly and bright tinsel decorated every picture that hung from the walls, and mistletoe hung at strategic points, throughout their living quarters.

This must be all Beauchamp's doing, but Hugo couldn't work out when the man had found the time and energy to transform the old place so, when he had so much extra work to attend to both today and tomorrow. He quickly abandoned his speculations on this subject when he heard a joyful yell from the drawing room, and found Lady Amanda there, on her knees in front of the fireplace, ripping paper off a large flat parcel.

'Oh, Hugo, just look at this! It's an antique blotter with silver cherubs on the front. I didn't even know Father Christmas was aware of how tatty my old one was getting. This is beautiful! I can hardly wait to write a letter, so that I can use it. What have you got Hugo? Come along, old chap, get ripping. You've got quite a few parcels to open.'

Hugo's gaze turned to where he had hung his 'stocking' last night; in actuality, a linen pillow slip with a card pinned to it, which bore his name. It was bulging with angled parcels and boxes, and the excitement that he had felt at this season so long ago now filled him again. He had, indeed, been transformed into a little boy.

Taking down the pillow slip and putting it on a sofa, he began to remove gifts from it, and unwrap them; first slowly, as one is taught to do in a polite way, then more vigorously, as one would like to do with every present one is ever given, but forbidden to by the dictates of good manners.

By the time he had a pile of discarded wrapping paper round his feet, the sofa held the components that comprised a complete train set, with all the fun little items that went with it: little signal boxes, a miniature station with its personnel, tiny passengers and sundry suitcases, miniature trees, a humped shape that was a tunnel, a level-crossing, complete with gates: there seemed to be endless little bits and pieces with which to construct a railway world.

'How did he know?' asked Hugo, flabbergasted, but hugely impressed.

'How did who know what?' enquired Lady Amanda, holding up a sparkling pair of earrings to the light.

'Beauchamp. And that I never had my own train set. I always had to ask my older brother's permission to use his, and he hardly ever said yes – at least, not until I had agreed to let him give me a Chinese burn, which was horrible.'

At that precise moment, he became aware of Beauchamp at the side of the sofa, and jumped slightly. 'Golly, you're just like a character in a pantomime – rather appropriate at this time of year. What can I do for you, Beauchamp?'

'Nothing. I just wanted to let sir know that I utilised an old wooden table, covered it with baize, and it now resides in the great hall, should you wish to play with your new acquisition.'

'Beauchamp, you are a miracle on two legs. There's nothing I'd like to do more,' replied Hugo, looking quite young again.

'By the way,' interjected Lady A, 'what did I get you for Christmas?' she asked. knowing that he always chose his own present.

'A micro-scooter of the highest quality, my lady. So convenient for getting around all the long corridors in such a substantial residence with efficiency and speed. And jolly good fun it is too,' he replied, with a smile of satisfaction on his lips. Christmas has the ability to bring out the child in everyone, even someone as stolid and reliable as Beauchamp.

'I believe it would be in order to open the rest of your

presents before commencing on setting out your track,' the manservant advised him, disappearing as suddenly as he had arrived, leaving the two elderly children to re-enact their childhoods in peace.

Hugo's next parcel contained a railway guard's hat, and the next one, a whistle on a sturdy piece of cord, so that he could properly control the running of his new railway service. 'I say, Manda! I don't know where you got Beauchamp, but he's an absolute diamond geezer, if you'll excuse my use of the vernacular.'

'I've actually no idea where Mama got him,' she replied, rubbing the material of a cashmere scarf against her cheek with approval. 'He just appeared after I came home from school for the last time; as a boot boy, in those days, and he's just been here ever since. I know we never deserved him, but he's stuck with the family through thick and thin, and I really don't know how I would manage without him. He goes above and beyond the call of duty as a matter of course, and in an emergency, he simply works miracles.'

Enid Tweedie arrived just after they got back from church, a guest for Christmas lunch, as it would give her a change from looking at her sister's miserable face and her mother's evil countenance, both of which she must have had to observe every Christmas of her life so far. She was going to be helping with tomorrow's affair, and Lady Amanda had decided that the only way to say a proper thank you was for her to join them for Christmas lunch.

She arrived in a swirl of snow, the like of which had been gently falling since the early hours, and now had reached a rather respectable two to three inches – enough not to hinder walking too much, but sufficient to proclaim the rare occurrence of a white Christmas. Standing on the doorstep with a sprig of holly (with berries) pinned to the lapel of her best coat, and a sprig of mistletoe attached, in an ambitiously racy way, to her hat, Lady Amanda looked at her old employee and friend as she stood there, snowflakes melting on her coat, and felt a wave of affection wash over her.

This woman too had stuck with her through thick and thin, giving her time generously at the drop of a hat, and had even acted as an undercover detective for her earlier in the year. How much more could you ask of a friend, and yet Lady Amanda had treated her, for most of that time, like a hired dogsbody. Feeling the prickle of a tear at her eye, she decided it must be time for a sherry, to drown this flood of sentimentality that had suddenly overtaken her.

For a moment, she had the revelation that it must be the unusual company of an old friend, in the shape of Hugo, this morning as she opened her presents, sharing her excitement and appreciation, that had made her look on Enid in a new light, but a couple of glasses of sherry would soon cure that, and a couple of cocktails would definitely see her back to normal.

'How did you get here this morning?' she asked, not having seen Enid's bicycle outside.

'Well, I thought you sent him,' she replied, enigmatically.

'Sent whom?' Lady Amanda had done absolutely no 'sending' today whatsoever.

'Beauchamp. He knocked on my door just as I was about to leave, and said he'd come to save me the journey in the snow. He said he didn't want me either slipping off my bicycle, or falling over and hurting myself.'

'Well, I'll be blowed. I simply didn't think about it Enid, but Beauchamp really has been your knight in shining armour this morning, hasn't he?'

At this information, Enid blushed, and slipped the sprig of mistletoe from her hat and popped it into her handbag. Maybe today was her lucky day.

After taking her outer clothes, Lady Amanda led her

into the drawing room where, from under the tree, she collected three presents, and thrust them into Enid's arms with a gruff, 'Merry Christmas, old friend.' Enid's face was a picture of surprise and delight, as she viewed the parcels now nestling in her arms.

'You shouldn't have, Lady Amanda,' she exclaimed, with a face that expressed the exact opposite.

'Little thank you for what you did for us when we were tangled up in those murders, earlier in the year. Got to reward our undercover agent for all her hard work,' replied Lady A, looking a little embarrassed. 'Go on, then, open them.'

Enid sat down on a chaise longue and delicately began to remove the wrapping paper, prompting a question from Hugo. 'Why are you doing it so carefully, Enid?'

'So that I can iron it and use it again,' came the automatic reply. Enid was too absorbed in not letting the sticky tape damage the pattern on the paper, even to think what she was saying.

As his mouth opened, to urge her to let herself go and just rip it off, he was stilled by a glare from Lady Amanda, who knew how important little savings like this were to Enid's life. She was not impoverished by any means, but the habits instilled in childhood had not died in Enid's psyche, and it was a matter of pride to her to let nothing go to waste unnecessarily.

From the first parcel she pulled a beautiful Italian leather handbag, exclaiming with delight, and reading out loud from the label. ''From Hugo, with all best wishes.' Why Mr Hugo, what a lovely present, but it looks awfully expensive.'

Hugo's mouth gaped, as he had, until now, had no inkling that such a gift from him existed. Lady Amanda came to his rescue by tipping him a discreet wink and explaining, 'Hugo knows how ladies love their handbags, and he wanted you to have something lovely but practical.'

'How thoughtful. I wouldn't have considered that such a notion would cross a man's mind. It's absolutely lovely, and I shall enjoy using it immensely. Thank you, Mr Hugo.'

'The second gift revealed a pair of silk scarves, one in spring colours, the other in autumn tints. 'Oh, Lady Amanda! You shouldn't have done, but they're beautiful.'

'Get on and open the other one, Enid. I'm dying to see what's in it,' she lied, for she had been the inspiration behind all three of these surprises.

'I'm doing my best, but there seems to be rather a lot of tape on this one, for the size of it. Hang on, there we go,' gushed Enid, now thoroughly enjoying herself with these hithertofore unheard of seasonal offerings. 'Why, what a beautiful purse! And so practical, with all those sections. And I don't think I've ever felt such soft leather, apart from gloves. But who's it from? *Beauchamp*?' she cried, with surprise, then her face fell, and she added in a small voice, 'But I've brought nothing for any of you.'

'We don't give to receive, Enid, dear. These are a token of our appreciation for all the hard work you do here, without the slightest murmur of complaint, and for the help you gave us in our little adventure. Enjoy them and think of us when you use them. Nobody could ask for more in return, than that.' Lady Amanda really knew how to schmooze when it was necessary.

A gong sounded in the hallway, and the three of them adjourned to the dining room where an impeccably laid table now held the various serving dishes necessary for the meal, and a great carving dish on which nestled a medium-sized turkey, a guinea fowl, a pheasant, and three quail. Beauchamp did like to provide a choice, and was even happier if everyone asked for a little of each, for that meant that he had chosen his viands successfully.

The meal passed with a little more liveliness than it usually did, and this was all down to the presence of Enid.

When she uncovered the parson's nose on her plate – maybe it was the three glasses of wine that she had already consumed that was the cause of her reaction – she laughed so hysterically that she ended up with hiccoughs, and her conversation throughout the rest of the main course was laced with small explosions from her diaphragm, and profuse apologies for the interruptions.

'Ab – hic-solutely deli-hic-ious birds – hic! I don't th-hic-ink I've ever ta-hic-sted some of these be-hic-fore. You must let me know wh-hic-at they are-hic.'

This set Lady Amanda and Hugo giggling, mainly at the surprised expression on her face whenever she interrupted her words and, here again, it was probably because, by now, they had caught up with her wine consumption, and all three were neck and neck.

There was an interesting hiatus during the pudding, when Enid started to choke on a silver sixpence; one of many that had graced the Golightly Christmas puddings since these particular coins had been made of sterling silver. Fortunately, Beauchamp knew how to administer the Heimlich manoeuvre, grabbed her swiftly from her seat like a rag doll, and carried out the coup de grace, producing a projectile that bounced across the table and landed back on the pudding plate, a feat so unlikely that none of them could believe it.

So far through the meal (and the wine) were they, however, that no one had the sharpness of mental capacity to calculate the odds of this happening. It also cured Enid's hiccoughs, and she sat down at her place again, grateful for Beauchamp's intervention.

'Nice try!' announced Lady A, swaying contentedly as she sipped from her glass.

'What do you mean, nice try?' asked Enid, unable to follow the thought processes that had produced this incomprehensible statement.

'Well, I thought you were trying for a Christmas Day

visit to the hospital, just to wish all the staff you know the complim-iments of the sea-season, 'n-all that,' – a brave attempt by Lady A to keep her speech coherent, but a little unsuccessful towards the end.

This produced more helpless laughter from Enid, and she replied, with difficulty, 'S-silly wo-woman. Anyone would thin-ink I spent ha-ha-ha-half, ha ha ha ha ha, my life in the hostipal. Ooh, whoopsadaisy! Bu' you know wha' I mean, don' you?'

Beauchamp made the brave decision, at that point, to abandon the cheese board and port, and the coffee and liqueurs, and suggested, in quite a forceful way, that they would be better off retiring to their rooms for a little lie down, after all the excitement (wine). Enid was welcome to have a rest in one of the guest rooms that was already made up and ready for occupation, should she agree.

Enid agreed. So did Lady Amanda. And Hugo. With alacrity. To each, the other two appeared blurred, therefore, they concluded, in their fuddled state, that the other two must be drunk, but they wouldn't mind a little time-out themselves. Thus it was agreed, and they left the dining room, Beauchamp supporting Enid on his arm, for the oblivion and recuperative qualities of the small death that is sleep.

At four-thirty, Beauchamp eventually retired to his own quarters to partake of his own Christmas meal, glad of the break and the fact that no one would ring for him for at least an hour. Tomorrow was going to be a very busy day, and he needed any rest he could manage to wangle today, to face the rigours of the Boxing Day experiment.

The rest of the day passed quietly, with only half-hearted nibbles attempted at the Christmas cake produced at teatime, the only liquids consumed during the afternoon and evening being several pots of tea and a large jug of Beauchamp's home-made lemonade. This was just as well, considering what the morrow would bring.

Chapter Nine
The Experiment Ends in Murder

Edith, with the loan of a flannelette nightie and a spare toothbrush (from Beauchamp's supply of same, for emergency use) had stayed the night for the first time in her acquaintance with Lady Amanda, and appeared at the breakfast table the next morning bright and breezy, and ready for whatever the day would bring. She could get to work earlier than if she had had to make the journey from home, as there was no public transport today, and she would have had need of her ancient bicycle to make the journey in the snow.

Lady Amanda, after an early night and a long sleep, was in sparkling form, fairly crackling with anticipation as she considered the task ahead of her. Hugo, on the other hand, was unusually pessimistic, and gave it as his opinion, over the bacon and eggs, that persuading a bunch of people that they had seen little of for quite some time, and didn't regularly socialise with, to support their venture, was a waste of time, energy and money.

'Come on, Hugo! Where's your spirit? Where's your hunger for a challenge? We can do this standing on our heads if we just summon our natural social graces and powers of persuasion. Look at that time you persuaded Daddy to line the parapets with fireworks for New Year's Eve. He was dead against the idea until you'd worked on him for a while.' Lady A had to spark his enthusiasm somehow.

'And regretted it afterwards. It took the fire brigade quite a time to put out all the little fires it started up on the roof, and he took rather a wigging from the chief fire officer afterwards, for doing such a foolish thing during a very dry winter. The fires very nearly broke through to the attics, and then where would you have been? Faced with a huge roofing bill, without their valiant efforts; that's where you would have been.'

'Don't be such a party-pooper, Hugo. It gave Daddy just the opportunity he needed to get that old roof sorted out, and all at the expense of the insurance company. Anyway, he never told you, but he just souped-up a few of those fireworks, so that he would get the desired result.'

Hugo's mouth went slack. 'You mean he used me as a pawn in a game of "fleece the insurance company"?'

'Of course he did. He thought you knew.'

'I had no idea. I've carried the guilt of the damage I thought I'd caused ever since.'

'Silly, silly Hugo. I thought you knew Daddy better than that. Anyway, perk yourself up. We may not have seen these people for a long time, but we used to have some damned fine times with them, and I hope that today will just be the first in another round of fun for all of us.'

'May I see the guest list, please, Lady Amanda?' asked Enid, who always like to know people's names, so that she didn't have to go through the embarrassing procedure of having to ask who they were.

'In my desk, Enid. Top drawer, under my diary. Help yourself. Hang around as I admit them, if you like, and that'll help you when it comes to remembering who's who. There're not coming until two o'clock, so you've got plenty of time to commit their names to memory.

The morning, not unsurprisingly, was spent rehearsing the tour part of the afternoon's proceedings, and the doors of all the rooms that they were unwilling to have other folk poke around in, were securely locked against any unwelcome invaders.

The plan was to give everyone a drink to welcome

them to the establishment, then take them on what Lady Amanda considered to be the 'below stairs' tour, to include the kitchens, scullery, buttery, brewery and wash room, downstairs, then to ascend to the second floor where the servants had their sleeping quarters. Beauchamp, being more familiar with the domestic running of the house during his employment, had volunteered to conduct the tour, pointing out items of interest on the way, and telling stories from the old days which had been passed down to him by long-gone members of staff.

He would leave tea laid out in the library, with the exception of the delicacies which had to be freshly produced, Lady Amanda would accompany him to add her two-penn'orth of interesting figures and facts, and Enid and Hugo would make the tea at a given signal (one bong on the gong on the half-landing to the first floor) to commence this task.

Beauchamp forbade anyone to enter the kitchen during the morning, and flew about its confines like a blue-arsed fly, getting the tasty morsels prepared. Lady Amanda consulted a notebook in which she had noted the 'off-the-cuff' stories with which she would flesh-out the bones of Beauchamp's prose, and with this, she prowled her kingdom (or queendom, which may be more apt, but isn't actually a real word), mouthing the tales she would tell, with appropriate facial expressions and arm and body movements, even going so far as to feign laughter in complete silence, at a joke she would make at a certain point in the proceedings..

Enid armed herself with a long-handled feather duster and a polishing cloth, and prowled every available room with this weapon, fighting a last-minute war with dust and the like, so that no one should get the impression that the household was slovenly in its care of the house. She was deadly with a duster, and nothing escaped her eagle eye, so long had she been eradicating this particular arch-enemy.

While this hive of activity swarmed around him, Hugo took himself off to the library, selected a book from the more modern shelves of the room's contents, and settled down, contentedly, to read. His excuse was that his knee was giving him particular trouble, and as he did not have an appointment to see the orthopaedic consultant until after the New Year, nobody could question the veracity of his tale.

At seven minutes to two, all three of them stood in the entrance hall, like sprinters at the start of the race of their lives. The whole house stood in silence, holding its breath for the moment where it would be put to the test.

At the sound of a car backfiring a good quarter of a mile away on the main road, they all visibly started, Enid going so far as to issue a squeak of surprise. 'Calm, troops,' ordered Lady Amanda, who was steeling herself to be nice to people. 'Best smiles to the fore, small-talk loaded and ready to fire.'

The sound of the bell ringing, at two minutes to the hour, almost caused the timid Enid to faint clean away, but Lady Amanda trod on her foot (accidentally on purpose) in her anxiety to be the first to greet her guests, and that brought her back to a state of being fully alert and ready for anything, including taking particular care where she put her feet. Lady Amanda was no slip of a girl, and she didn't want to spend the rest of the busy afternoon with a broken toe or two.

Lt Col. Aloysius Featherstonehaugh-Armitage and his wife Angelica were the first to arrive and Lady Amanda, in her excitement at the commencement of her battle plan, forgot to address them formally for Enid's benefit, and merely bade them welcome with the words, 'How lovely to see you again after such a long time, Stinky. How's the family, Donkey? All prospering, I trust?'

As they crossed the threshold, Beauchamp stepped forward to take their coats, hats, and gloves, and the residents of Belchester Towers had their first opportunity to take a look at what had happened to the grounds since they had last been outside. Lady Amanda opened the large doors wide and surveyed the iced lawns and bedecked shrubs and trees, as her guests stamped their feet on the (fortunately large) doormat to rid themselves of the encrustations of snow they had gathered on their walk from their car.

'Can't remember when we last had a white Christmas,' exclaimed Lady Amanda, clapping her hands together with glee. 'Perhaps we could all have a snowball fight on the lawn after tea.'

Totally ignoring the scandalised expressions on her first two guests' faces, she turned to them with a winning smile and urged Beauchamp to accompany them to the drawing room where a large fire burned, so that they could defrost before they had a little drink. She had obviously made up for her gaffe about snowballs by this remark, and Stinky and Donkey smiled in approval at the idea of a winter warmer at such an early hour. It was, after all, a bank holiday, and the sun and the yard-arm would have nothing to do with protocol today.

As all the clocks in the house chimed the hour, there was another smart knock on the door, which opened this time to admit Sir Jolyon and Lady Felicity *ff*olliat DeWinter. Sir Jolyon was red of face, even from the short walk he had taken from the car to the front door, and his complexion wasn't aided by the air temperature. Although the sun was shining, it was bitterly cold, with a slow lazy north wind that sliced at one like knives.

Lady Felicity merely looked like a child wearing an older person's skin, and skipped into the house babbling happily about how delighted they had been to receive Lady Amanda's invitation, and how much they had been looking forward to such an unusual experience. Beauchamp relieved her of her mink coat, hat, and fur-trimmed gloves, scandalised to hear Sir Jolyon call after him, 'You make sure you take care of that coat. It's not ranch mink, my man; it's the real wild article. Just make sure it doesn't bite you!' The manservant bore them away, with a scowl of fury at being so addressed, to some below-stairs region where such things resided while guests were in occupation. "My man"! Whatever next? 'Oi, buddy', perhaps?

Search as she might, over the years, Lady Amanda had never been able to solve the mystery of what Beauchamp did with all the coats, and had finally given up the impossible task of discovering his hiding place. Maybe the man had access to another dimension, where all menservants hid such bulky items during family entertainments. She just hoped he didn't decide to stay there, today, after such a blow to his dignity and elevated position.

Blimp escorted himself to the drawing room, anxious as he was to warm his backside at the fire, and when Beauchamp returned to accompany Fifi, she was still prattling away happily to herself about how lovely everything was, and how much she was looking forward to seeing the others invited for the occasion, hoping that she would already know some of them. The manservant at her side nodded his head in attentive agreement with much that she said, without even being aware that he was doing it. Such a habit had it become, that his mind was in the kitchen, running over all the preparations, to check that nothing had been neglected.

'Henry! Hilda! What a pleasure to see you again!' trilled Lady Amanda as a third couple arrived on the doorstep. She had picked up her game, and was using their real names now, so that Enid could chalk-up a house-point by addressing them as such, without having to be introduced. Although she wasn't using their full names, she was at least giving Enid sufficient evidence to work out who was who, and had only blundered over the first arrivals.

Cutie and Daisy were next, and each received a warm handshake and a kiss on the cheek, as Lady Amanda chortled, 'Sir Montacute! Lady Margaret! How delightful that you could attend our little entertainment this afternoon.'

The penultimate couple to enter Belchester Towers that afternoon was the Mapperley-Mintos, who actually commented on Lady Amanda using their given names. 'Given up on Monty and Maddie then, have you, Manda? Too grown-up for all that stuff, now, eh?'

'Not at all,' gushed Lady Amanda. 'I just thought that you might think it childish of me to use the diminutives of so long ago.'

'Not at all,' growled Monty. 'Still use them ourselves, as a matter of fact. Go back to that now, shall we?'

'With pleasure, Monty,' replied their hostess, noticing out of the corner of her eye that Enid had placed herself just out of the arriving guests' sightline, and was making copious notes on her list of those invited for the occasion. She'd get it right. She'd cudgel them into her memory, until she couldn't get it wrong if she tried. Very tenacious, was Enid.

Last to arrive by a good five minutes, and causing some little consternation in the troops that manned the line by the front door, were Capt Leslie and Mrs Lesley Barrington-Blyss, the former looking a tad out of sorts, the latter, with a worried smile on her face. Porky, as Mrs B-B was known, made profuse apologies for their tardy arrival, citing a domestic staff crisis just before they had left. While she did this, she kept one hand behind her back, her stout fingers crossed to negate the lie.

Beauchamp took their outer clothes, while Porky clung possessively to a large tapestry handbag. 'Why on earth have you brought that monstrosity with you? Surely you haven't brought your knitting?' her husband asked, glaring at the bag with disgust, as she opened it to insert her gloves for safe-keeping. 'Why don't you go the whole hog, Porky, and wear a damned rucksack, but I can assure you'll be walking alone, for I won't be seen with you' he concluded, in withering tones,' then added, 'Whole hog – Porky! I say, that was rather a good one, wasn't it? Haha! Hahahahaha!'

Neither Beauchamp nor Lady A, though, seemed amused by this comment, made in extremely dubious taste, but, instead of an angry retort from Porky, a small smile of triumph appeared on her face. Why, though, she should be so pleased that she had annoyed him in front of others, was inexplicable. Maybe it was the sour look that she, Amanda, had bestowed upon him that had pleased Porky, thought Lady A. Popeye wasn't the most popular man in the county, nor ever would be, but he'd better tread carefully – Porky was his only ally at the moment, God bless her, and she'd stuck with him through thick and thin, even with this awful book business. She really was a good and loyal soul.

What she didn't know, however, was that Porky and Popeye had, in fact, had a rather heated discussion – row – about whether to attend at all. Popeye had stated categorically that he wanted to stay in his study and work on his book, which was nearly ready for publication. His publisher had sent him a series of instructions for where he wanted changes made, and small rewrites, and he wanted to get it finished as soon as possible, to get the book hurried on to the bookshelves. Never mind how much embarrassment and trouble he caused for others; he just wanted the notoriety.

The money would be damned useful too, for he was sick of penny-pinching in these hard times, even though he'd had to pursue a less than traditional route to get his work before the public gaze, and he just hoped that the risk would pay off. He'd warned her that, should it not sell extremely well, they might have to consider moving to a smaller property and dispensing with what little domestic help they currently enjoyed, and this had left Porky in a cleft stick.

She had finally justified putting her rather pudgy foot down over the matter by telling him that he might make some very useful contacts from the afternoon, as they had no idea who else had been invited, and that, furthermore, if he didn't comply, he'd become known as an untrustworthy, ill-mannered cur, throughout the County set. She'd make sure of that!

All her guinea pigs safely gathered in, Lady Amanda escorted the late-comers into the drawing room where she was pleased to find that Beauchamp had already taken orders for drinks and was, at this very moment, handing them round to those who had arrived more promptly. The man was a veritable gem.

'... hook from which the meat hung, behind this sheet of semi-circular metal ... a device for cutting the Seville oranges for marmalade-making ... a wash-dolly with which the laundry maid would agitate the clothes ... copper moulds for all sorts of puddings, both shapes, custards and ices ... the hard wooden beds on which the servants slept ... the wooden staircase which the female staff ascended to their rooms ... the marble wash-stands where they had to wash in cold water every morning ...'

Beauchamp led the party into the library at the end of the tour, looking as fresh as the proverbial daisy. Lady Amanda brought up the rear, looking as if she had been into battle, but quickly pushed her hair back into place, fixed a big social smile on her face, and entered the room which was now scented with some of the delights of which they were about to partake.

Not even a torturer from the Inquisition could make her

confess how exhausted she felt, traipsing round the unfamiliar quarters that had been occupied, in her childhood and for many years before, by the staff, nor the horror she had felt when she had taken a good, hard look at how they had lived. Cleaning the quarters up had not done this for her, but today had, and she thanked her lucky stars that she had been born into the layer of society that she had.

Beauchamp had disappeared as soon as he had reached the library, now at work in the kitchen, no doubt on the things that had to be served either fresh, or warm, and her guests were gathered round the big library table helping themselves to delicate morsels of food. Enid and Hugo had done their job as promised, and two large silver teapots, one each of Indian and China, stood on mats on the table, to assuage their guests' thirst after their portion of enforced education for the day.

Lady Amanda sank into the confines of a porter's chair, and hid herself for a moment, to give herself a few seconds to summon up fresh energy and enthusiasm. That they enjoyed their afternoon tea was tantamount to the success of her venture, but that they felt relaxed enough to stay on for cocktails and give her some decent feedback was just as vital, and she must remain the perfect hostess, throughout the experience.

Finally rising from her hideaway, she poured a cup of the restoring Indian infusion for herself, put some choice morsels on her plate and began to circulate amongst her guests. No one seemed at all put out by anything, and they looked as if they were having a jolly time of snooping round a neighbour's home. Well, she had an extra card up her sleeve that would make their day.

'Excuse me, everyone,' she announced after about twenty minutes. 'Today my home is at your service. Should any of you wish to explore its other rooms, those that constitute, I suppose, upstairs, please feel free to do so over the next hour or so. Beauchamp will be your guide, should you require him. At that point, I should be grateful for any comment on what I propose to do, and you will all be very welcome to stay on for cocktails.'

Hugo, suddenly coming to life, called out, 'Why don't we get Beauchamp to light a yule log in the great hall and turn this occasion into an out-and-out party, everyone? He's a domestic marvel, and I'm sure he could rustle up enough grub for us all. A bowl of punch and a bit of music would liven us all up a bit, and we could make this a red-letter day. After all, we haven't seen each other in an absolute age, have we?'

Enthusiastic mutterings greeted this suggestion, and as the guests made themselves ready to vacate the library, discarding cups and saucers, and plates empty of everything except a few crumbs, in preparation for having a good old nose around Belchester Towers, Hugo was unaware of Lady Amanda's approach until she suddenly landed next to him on the sofa, making him squeal in pain as the jolt shuddered through the joints he was still waiting to have replaced.

'I say, old thing, that was a bit rough, wasn't it?' he asked, trying to draw himself away from her encroaching bulk, as all the bits of her settled into place with a little help from gravity.

'And throwing my home open to this bunch of social vultures for a full-blown party isn't? Really, Hugo, I don't know how you have the bare-faced cheek to do something like that, when I've been running around like a headless chicken all day, and all you've done is sit around on your bum and rest your poor old joints. Making extra work for other people on a day like today is just beyond the pale, and you know it.'

Hugo had the grace to look shame-faced, but defended himself by saying, 'I thought everyone was having such a jolly good time that it would be just like the old days, with some of the old crowd here to recreate the atmosphere.'

'Do you actually remember "carriages at three"? It was deadly! One hardly ever saw daylight, and entered a twilight existence that was just one round of parties. A single one of those would be the death of me now. I just hope that a good snoop round, followed by a few drinks and a good old bitch about our set-up here will be enough for all of them. I forbid you to tell Beauchamp to light a yule log in the great hall, or forage around for enough food for well over a dozen people.'

'Sorry, Manda. I must have been temporarily astray from my wits. I had forgotten that morning-after feeling, and I think the consequences would be much greater at my age. If anyone says anything, I'll tell them I'm getting a bit senile. Will that do you?'

'Just be honest, and say that your enthusiasm carried you away for a moment. We don't need them spreading the news around the county that Hugo Cholmondley-Crichton-Crump is going off his chump, now do we?'

'You're right, as always. Shall we retire to the drawing room for a little peace and quiet, while they're all off moaning that they can't get access to our underwear drawers?'

'Just a minute,' she requested, and, turning from Hugo, she called in a very loud voice, 'If you would all follow Beauchamp, he will do the rounds of the tour with you, as he knows so much more of all the interesting nooks and crannies of this place than I do. When the tour is finished, feel free to take yourselves where you will and have a good old explore. I'll be very interested to hear what you have to say later, when I ask you for some feedback. And don't forget the cocktails! Have a good time!'

'Now,' she turned back to her house-mate. 'You had just made a most excellent suggestion, and one I think we ought to act on, on the instant. What about you, Enid?' she called, seeing her house-guest enter the library to carry away some of the crockery and the few morsels of uneaten food out to the kitchen.

'I'm fine, Lady Amanda. I'll just finish this clearing away, while Beauchamp is conducting everyone round the nooks and crannies, and when he gets back from showing them the public and family rooms, I shall help him with the washing up, then I expect we'll have a nice cup of tea at the kitchen table. I seem to have upset one of your guests, however,' she concluded.

'How on earth could you have done that?' asked Lady Amanda, surprised that such a well-mannered and mild woman as Enid could make any impression on the elephants' hides that her old friends possessed.

'I think, although I'm not quite sure, that I had a bit of a 'Chumley' moment with that old army man with the moustache.'

'What on earth did you say to him?' asked Lady Amanda, wondering what sort of gaffe Enid had managed to make.

'I asked him if he was enjoying himself. I'd worked out who he was from my list, although I think you called him 'Stinky' when you let him in.'

'Yes, sorry about that. I was a little over-excited, and forgot that I was giving you clues to everyone's identity.'

'I addressed him by what I had assumed was his name, but when I used it he looked at me as if I were a snake ready to strike, and went off muttering to himself and snorting.'

'What did you call him, Enid?' asked Lady Amanda, knowing exactly what her friend was about to say.

'Lt Col. Featherstonehaugh-Armitage, of course.'

'And I suppose he went off muttering 'Fanshaw', did he?'

'That's exactly right, Lady Amanda. How on earth did you know? Although I think I already know the answer.'

'Because that's how his name's pronounced: Fanshaw-

Armitage.'

Enid sighed the sigh of someone tried beyond endurance. 'Well, I just wish he'd spell it that way then. What is it with your lot – sorry to sound coarse – that they can't just spell their names how they sound?'

'Sheer bloody-mindedness, I expect,' was the answer she received, and she must have been satisfied with it, because she trotted off to the kitchen, perfectly happy once more.

Lady Amanda and Hugo had had barely an hour of peace and quiet in which to snatch forty-winks, when a shriek, as piercing as that of a banshee, suddenly shattered the silence of the house.

Lady Amanda awoke with a 'Whaah!' of surprise, only to find that she had dribbled all down her cardigan while she had been 'resting her eyes'. Hugo, not so tired from the day's exertions, as there hadn't been any for him, was already up and heading for the door before she shook herself fully awake. 'What the hell's going on?' she asked, rubbing discreetly at her front with her handkerchief.

The screaming carried on, occasionally interspersed with the long drawn-out wail of 'Muuurdeeer!'

With Hugo now at her heels, having been overtaken, she sped towards the source of the distress calls, when Beauchamp suddenly appeared in front of her and uttered the words, 'I'm sorry to inform you, my lady, that there is a body in the library. I'm afraid that one of your guests has been the victim of a murderous attack.'

Heading directly to the library, without stopping to pass 'Go' or collecting £200, Lady Amanda punched a fist in the air and called over her shoulder, 'Yes, Virginia, there is a Santa Claus!' Hugo, who had not watched the right films to explain what she was talking about, merely limped along in her wake, trying to summon up sufficient energy to keep up with her.

Chapter Ten
An Inspector Calls

Inspector Moody was not in the best of moods. In fact, it would be more accurate to state that Inspector Moody was in an absolutely diabolical mood. There he had been, his sister and family gathered round his dining table playing their annual game of Monopoly, his wife struggling in the kitchen to assemble enough turkey sandwiches for the whole brood of them, when his telephone had shrilled, and extinguished the flame of pride that always burned in his heart when he put up Susan and her brood, and treated them to the benefit of his entertaining expertise.

The call had come out of the blue, and when the nature of the crime had been partnered with the residence of Lady Amanda Golightly, Moody had turned a very odd colour. Mrs Moody would not have been surprised to see smoke issuing from his ears. She knew that expression very well, and was always grateful when she was not on the receiving end of it.

He was still grinding his teeth when PC Glenister arrived at the house to collect him, and his whole family gave a collective sigh of relief and gratitude when he disappeared through the door, informing them that he had no idea when he would be back, and hoped that he made it back home without committing murder himself. That certainly left them with something to chew over in his absence.

Now, he found himself in the library at Belchester Towers, staring down at the lifeless body of Capt Leslie

Barrington-Blyss, his head slumped forward on the library table. 'So, what did this poor chap do? Criticise your mince pies?' he asked, throwing a glare in Lady Amanda's direction.

'I had nothing whatsoever to do with this, Inspector. He was perfectly all right when I last saw him about an hour and a half ago. There must be a maniac on the loose. Have you had any reports of someone wandering off from Speedwell?'

This, as Inspector Moody was well aware, was the local psychiatric hospital, and he wasn't going to let this new sparring partner get away with blaming a perfectly respectable mental health facility, that did a very sound job of securing the establishment and its grounds, for something that she was obviously responsible for.

'There have been no such reports. And don't you think this is a gross case of overkill? Are any of your guests out of their minds, or subject to psychotic episodes?' If she could besmirch Speedwell, then he could return the slur, by implicating one of this bunch of Hooray Henrys and Henriettas.

'Overkill, Inspector? Would you kindly explain yourself this instant? I have no idea what you are babbling about, and how dare you insult my guests!'

'Have you taken a close look at the deceased ... m' lady?' he asked, the last one and a half words nearly choking him, and causing his face to empurple quite alarmingly. He didn't see why he should kowtow to this interfering old windbag, just because she had some sort of minor title. She had been a thorn in his side once, and he didn't want to find himself worrying at the same spot again, at the end of the year.

'I have been too busy summoning you, comforting his widow, and dissipating the air of panic that was present when he was discovered. Pray, share your more intimate knowledge with me, so that I may render a proper opinion.' She could be haughty when she chose, and she wasn't going to be intimidated by this lump of a man, whom she considered had the intellect of a flagstone.

'If you would care to take a closer visual evaluation, you may note that a blow to the back of the head seems to have been administered – note the bloody wound. An examination of his neck will show signs of a garrotte having being used on him, as it is still in place, and if you examine his throat, you will notice that, just below the still present garrotte, it has been cut from ear to ear. Anyone who wasn't half-blind would notice the knife sticking out between his shoulder blades, and from the colour of his lips and the slight odour issuing from his mouth, I would hazard a fairly confident guess that he has been poisoned as well.

'Is this some sort of Christmas joke that you're all playing, because if it is, not only is it not funny and in the most appalling taste, but someone is going to spend an awfully long time in prison for what has happened here today. I will not be taunted like this!'

As the inspector came to the end of his descriptive accusation, he had worked himself up into such a state of fury that spittle had gathered at the corners of his mouth, and collected in a very unpleasant and not at all refined fine froth. Beauchamp handed him a tissue without a word.

'I thoroughly resent what you're implying about my old friends here. Murder is no joking matter, and should not be treated as such. I'm sure that each and every one of us is willing to co-operate to the fullest with your enquiries, to bring whoever did this to justice. Now, if you could just act like a gentleman for a moment, and not carry on like an hysterical teenager, maybe we can begin this investigation.'

'Are you implying that I am not acting in a professional manner?' asked Moody, looking as if he could turn nasty again.

'If the shoe fits, Inspector ...' Lady Amanda let this hang in the air, and saw PC Glenister trying to suppress a smile. As he caught her gaze, he winked at her, and she suspected that she had an ally in the making in this young man.

Remembering the first foray into murder investigation that she and Hugo had made when the latter had moved into Belchester Towers, she reckoned that with this chap 'on side' they had a far better chance of beating Moody to the solution.

At last she had admitted why things had seemed so humdrum. She had been longing for the excitement of detecting again, the call of adventure, and the investigation of the unknown. It had added a liberal sprinkling of spice to her existence, and now she felt she couldn't live without it.

She and Hugo would tackle this murder and, come hell or high water, they would identify the murderer before that small-minded little inverted snob could even scratch the surface of the truth. And if Hugo didn't want to play, he could stay behind in his playpen, while she went hither and thither searching for clues.

'I shall conduct my guests to the drawing room, Inspector Moody, while you seek to gather together your manners, and you may interview us one by one in the dining room. The table in there should prove perfect for taking notes. I shall also alert my manservant to expect a team of what I believe you call SOCOs, to take samples and suchlike from the scene, for forensic analysis.

'Should you or your men require any refreshments, just ring for Beauchamp, and he will oblige. Now, if you will excuse me, I must accompany my guests to less distressing surroundings.' With a strong sense of having put the man in his place, she gathered her old friends round her, and set off for the drawing room, requesting Beauchamp to bring them all a nice pot of tea, to settle everyone's nerves.

Inspector Moody, more out of spite than from any other motive, apprehended Beauchamp on his way to the kitchen to carry out his mission of mercy before he could obtain access to his over-sized kettle, and informed him that he would like to question him first.

'But I'm ordered to provide tea to soothe the guests' nerves. Some of them are undoubtedly suffering from shock,' he retorted, and got it; both barrels.

'I don't care if her ladyship has asked you to provide a priest for a dying child, matey. You're going nowhere until I've questioned you, and you can argue until you're blue in the face, and it won't make any difference. At the moment, I'm in charge, and I'd like that to be clear to everyone in this house this afternoon, including you, Jeeves. And if you refuse to co-operate, I shall arrest you for obstructing a policeman in the execution of his duty. Got that?

'Lady high-and-mighty Golightly might think herself mistress of all she surveys, but she, like every citizen of this country, is not above the law of the land, and today, I represent that law. What I say, goes, without question. Now, put that in your pipe and smoke it. And if Lady Muck doesn't like it, she can whistle! Comprende? Good! Now, siddown, and don't you dare to look down your nose at me, or I'll find something to charge you with; you see if I don't.'

'Very well, Inspector,' replied Beauchamp, with his very best manners polished to perfection. 'How may I be of assistance?'

PC Glenister was already seated at the dining room table, his notebook out, his pen poised, resembling nothing more than an eager puppy waiting for a stick to be thrown for him. He hadn't long come out of training and Belchester was his first posting. He'd thought it would be all lost dogs and cats, with perhaps a few pairs of knickers being stolen from clothes-lines thrown in, for a bit of spice, but it had not proved to be so.

In his first month as a fully-fledged police constable, Lady Amanda had whirled into the station with a tale of murder in a nursing home, and had beaten his boss to the finishing line, while Inspector Moody still thought there was no case to investigate. Now, here he was again, embroiled with the same energetic and enthusiastic old lady, and there had been another murder.

He suspected he was going to really enjoy this posting, and had a feeling that he would be working more closely with his current hostess than with his boss. Moody's name suited him, and anything a humble PC could do to solve a mysterious death in semi-aristocratic surroundings couldn't do said PC's career a jot of harm.

Beauchamp, another who was no fan of the inspector, extracted great enjoyment from informing that officer that during the time when the murder could have taken place, i.e. after the tour during the period when everyone was wandering around alone, he had spent the whole time in the kitchen with Enid Tweedie, dealing with the domestic fall-out caused by the rather large number of persons for afternoon tea, and, resentfully and reluctantly, the inspector had to let him go about his duty of providing tea for the drawing room.

PC Glenister was dispatched to fetch Lady Amanda, and when she entered the dining room, the inspector had daggers in his eyes. This overweight – fat, actually – old windbag with all her airs and graces, had defeated him once, and he was determined not to let that happen again. She might be a Lady, but he wasn't inclined to be a gentleman when dealing with this case. He would use every low-down trick he could think of to get to the perpetrator first. He would not be humiliated a second time by this bumbling old amateur.

'Sit down and let's get this over with,' he said in a commanding voice, his eyes as cold and hard as flints, as he gazed at this infuriating woman.

'So kind, Inspector,' she replied, giving him one of her most open smiles, and pulling out a dining chair. 'Will you and your constable be in need of any refreshment?'

PC Glenister's eyes lit up, but Moody merely glared at his hostess and declined the offer, without even the manners to have declared it a kind one.

'I want you to give me the goods on this lot you've got here. I want to know everything about them that may have given them a motive, and I don't want you to pull any punches. And if you don't co-operate, I'm going to have you down the station so fast, your feet won't touch the ground. A night in the cells will soon loosen your tongue,' he spat at her.

'How frightfully amusing of you, Inspector. I must tell the Chief Constable about your talent for doing impressions of a detective from a B-movie. Now, from what I understood of what you just said, you would like me to tell you anything about my friends that might be construed as a motive for murder. Is that correct?'

Moody was shocked into silence by what she had just declared, and merely nodded his head to the final part of it, while enquiring, 'You actually know the Chief Constable, then?'

'Of course I know old Roland. We've served on several committees together over the years. He can't be far off retirement now. I know he'll fight that tooth and nail. Very dedicated man. But as for my house guests, I haven't known them well since we were all much younger. We used to go around in a group with a few others. You know the sort of thing? Everyone invited to the same balls and dinners, you sort of end up as a little gang.'

Moody, of course, knew nothing of the sort. The only balls he had ever had anything to do with were footballs, and he had what he called his 'dinner' in the station canteen, at what he called dinnertime – about one p.m. His upbringing had been so different from hers that he might as well have been brought up on another planet, and he resented this deeply. She belonged to a world, part of which it was impossible for him to become. How dare she! He refused to feel inferior!

'I know Maddie used to smuggle bottles of sherry into her dorm – that's Mrs Madeleine Mapperley-Minto, PC Glenister. And, of course, there was that time – actually, I think it was twice – that Bonkers was caught raiding the jam cupboard at school; hand actually in the jar when he was busted by Mato. That's Col. Henry Heyhoe-Caramac, if you're taking notes. I don't think I've even been custodian of the knowledge of anything that has occurred, of a criminal nature, in their adult lives, however.

'I know I'm not being particularly helpful, but they're mostly a bunch of jolly good chaps, and I can't see any of them having a reason to commit murder, and in my house, too. I still stick to the theory that it was an escaped psychopath from the mad house up the road.'

'You must know something. Come on, spit it out, or I'll have to get tough with you.' Moody had temporarily forgotten about the Chief Constable.

'I can assure you that you could torture me with red-hot pokers, and I would not be able to deliver any further knowledge than I've already given you. You don't still do that, do you? I don't think I should like it very much.'

The woman was toying with him, and he'd gone as far as he could with his rudeness. There was nothing else to do but dismiss her from his sight, and hope that one of the other nobs would know more than she did about this whole sorry crew. Moody could be a very jealous man when he chose to be.

Hugo, on the other hand, had nearly driven the inspector into a state where he would have admitted himself as a voluntary patient at the local mental institution, with his tales about pranks and larks they had all got up to as teenagers, stopping to indulge in a wheezy laugh, as he got to the end of each story. He had managed to bumble on for about fifteen precious minutes of the 'golden time' after a murder, before Moody had actually stood up and held up his hand to halt the flow.

Without a word of explanation, he had merely said, in a strangled voice, 'Goodbye, sir. Send in the widow next!' and Hugo left feeling puzzled and unappreciated. Had he not unearthed every little episode of their early years that could have landed them in quite a lot of hot water? How ungrateful he had seemed, and he'd hardly paid attention at all. The PC, on the other hand, had scribbled away like nobody's business, sometimes smiling to himself as he struggled to keep up with the flow of anecdotes. Nice young man, that, he concluded, and went off to ask Porky to attend at the inspector's pleasure.

Mrs Lesley Barrington-Blyss arrived with a handkerchief clasped to her face to staunch the tears that sprang from her eyes. A bonny baby, she had grown into a chubby child, then a tubby teenager. Her weight had made her self-conscious, and meeting Capt Leslie when she had been a portly and definitely on-the-shelf adult, had been the only thing in her life that allowed her not to be distressed about how she looked.

She had never minded being called Porky, because she knew that her husband loved her just the way she was. She was now a majestically large woman, although light on her feet, and seemed to float along the ground rather than walk.

This afternoon she floated into the dining room, weeping copiously, and threw herself down into a dining chair which creaked ominously as she landed. 'Whatever am I going to do without my Popeye?' she hooted in distress, like a ship that has been holed below the waterline, and sending the inspector into a panic. What on earth was a 'Popeye'? As far as he was concerned, it was a sailor man, whose girlfriend was called Olive Oyl.

'Popeye?' he queried, wondering if the woman was crackers.

'My husband,' she replied through the cotton of her handkerchief. 'Leslie.'

She was at it again! Surely *her* name was Lesley. Inspector Moody cleared his throat self-consciously. He was already in the dark as to what a Popeye was, and now she was introducing herself as if she were a separate person from herself, as it were. And where on earth did her husband fit into all this gibberish? His thoughts may have been muddled, and he knew what he meant, but he had no idea what this lady was talking about? 'Lesley?' he queried, in a rather worried voice.

'My husband. We shared the same name, but spelled differently,' Mrs Barrington-Blyss explained, as if to a fool, without losing her place in her handkerchief.

Now Moody really was flummoxed. Of course they shared the same name. They were married. What in the name of God did Popeye and this other Lesley have to do with the dead man? Maybe she was on some sort of medication and hallucinated, or made up things that couldn't possibly be true.

He was just about to send her away until she was less hysterical, when Glenister approached him from behind and whispered in his ear, 'I think you'll find that they shared the same forename, and that he was called Popeye because he wore an eye-patch, and only had one eye. You may have noticed the patch in the library when we examined the body.'

Moody had done nothing of the sort in his fury at being summoned to Belchester Towers on Boxing Day, but in the situation in which he thought he had been embroiled, this information shone a great light on the events since Mrs Barrington-Blyss had entered the room. He glowered instinctively at Glenister, for having the temerity to interrupt him when he was questioning a possible suspect, but he was nevertheless intensely grateful for this enlightenment, although he would never admit it.

'I'm very sorry for your loss,' Moody began again, only to produce a fresh howl from the recent widow. 'And I should be very grateful if you would pull yourself together for a few minutes so that I can question you. I'm sure you want your husband's murderer caught as much as, if not even more than, I do.'

At the mention of the murder, Mrs Barrington-Blyss's sobs rose to a howl that suddenly transformed into hysterical laughter. Pulling the handkerchief from her face, she screamed with mirth, rocking backwards and forwards in her chair, tears shooting from her eyes as she did so. Moody was scandalised and not a little nonplussed. What on earth was he to do with a woman who appeared to find her husband's murder so highly amusing?

Louder sounds penetrated through to the drawing room, the door of which was not completely closed, and her laughter reached the others, foregathered there. 'I'd better go and give that ghastly little man a hand. He hasn't the nous to know what to do in a situation like this,' announced Lady A, rising from her seated position.

In the dining room, the door was suddenly flung open, Lady Amanda marched smartly into the room, stopping by Mrs B-B's chair, raised a hand and slapped her soundly on her left cheek. The ensuing silence was deafening. 'This woman is in no condition to be questioned. I am going to summon my own doctor, who can administer a sedative. Your constable here can take her home, and you can question her when she is in a fit state to think straight. Her husband's body is barely cold, and you expect her to be able to answer questions about it? Disgraceful, I call it!

'Constable Glenister, I should be grateful if you would drive Mrs Barrington-Blyss home, and I shall get

Beauchamp to follow you in the Rolls. He can then bring you back when the doctor has arrived to take care of her. I believe she has a housekeeper, so I assume she will not be alone tonight. Her health and mental state are more important, at the moment, than answering a few silly questions from the inspector here. Follow me, both of you,' she concluded, and led the way from the room, Constable Glenister and Lesley Barrington-Blyss following meekly in her wake, leaving Moody to twiddle his thumbs in solemn solitude.

Lady Amanda deposited the emotionally charged widow in Hugo's room, and moved to the hall to call Dr Campbell Andrew away from his Boxing Day festivities. This done, she found Beauchamp, as usual, at her shoulder when she wanted him, and explained the situation to him. All the while, Constable Glenister had stood by, a grin on his face at the way she had bested Moody, without even seeming to try, and in such a situation, that the inspector could hardly argue. What a woman!

As the door of Hugo's ground-floor bedroom shut behind Lady Amanda, Moody left the dining room and burst in on the rest of the party, demanding to speak to each of the other guests in turn. She could hardly ruin all of his attempts at questioning his prime suspects in the case.

Sir Jolyon *ff*olliat DeWinter took the lead, and rose to follow the man into the next room. Someone, after all, had to set an example and, most probably, put this uppity oik in his place. Sir Jolyon had gained the impression that the inspector suffered from a shortage of good manners, and anyone who could reduce good old Porky to such a pitiable condition needed to be taught a lesson, in his opinion, but he'd treat him as he found him – for now.

After the preliminary enquiries concerning name, address and contact numbers, of which Moody had, himself, to take note, as Glenister would obviously be gone for some time, the inspector began his questioning with, 'Have you any idea who may have had a motive for this murder?'

'Absolutely none,' replied Sir Jolyon. (*'The subject answered in the negative,'* scribbled Moody.)

'Can you tell me what you were doing at the time of the murder?' he continued.

'What time, exactly, would that be, old man?' queried Sir Jolyon, not being in possession of this snippet of information.

'Between the time the official guided tour ended, and the time Capt. Barrington-Blyss was discovered in a life-deprived condition in the library,' replied Moody, beginning to let his language blossom into purple blooms, and suspecting that Sir Jolyon was being purposely obstructive and time-wasting.

'Life-deprived – ha! Is that new police-speak, then? What's wrong with good old "dead"? And to answer your question, I went to the old ballroom where I spent many a happy hour in my youth. This time of year, and all that, can get one a bit nostalgic and sentimental, and I just wanted to bring back some of the sweet old memories.'

'I am reliably informed that the free time available to the group of guests was something in the order of an hour. Do you expect me to believe that you stood in an old ballroom reminiscing for a full sixty minutes?' Moody was well on the way to living up to his name.

'Believe what you like, old chap. That's what I did, and whether you choose to accept it as the truth, is neither here nor there. I'm not going to invent things just to make your job more interesting.'

'Can you produce any witnesses to this pensive period in the afternoon?' Moody was definitely up for a bit of a rumble with this pompous old twit.

'NO!' roared Sir Jolyon. 'Neither can I produce rabbits out of hats, nor doves out of handkerchiefs. I stood there for an hour recalling the past, and if my word's not good enough for you, you can take a running jump. You've already had poor Porky in hysterics, and now you're trying to goad me beyond endurance.

'I've know the deceased since Porky married him. We have never been close friends and I know little about him. Why on earth, that being the case, should I want to murder him; and so comprehensively, I might add?'

'My investigations will reveal anything that you do not admit to me during questioning.' Moody didn't think he was winning, but was willing to get a little heavier.

'You jumped-up little jobsworth! Your threats don't frighten me! As far as I'm concerned, you can stick your questioning where the monkey sticks his nuts, and bloody good luck to you. I'm going back to the drawing room, and, should you wish to speak to me again, I shall insist on my solicitor being present, if only to restrain me from committing common assault on a very common little man.'

After this uncompromising outburst, Sir Jolyon extracted a fat cigar from the inside pocket of his jacket, clipped the end, and lit it, blowing his first inhalation of smoke across the table, straight into the inspector's face. Then, without a by-your-leave, he stood up and left the room, his face a picture of someone who is having problems with his haemorrhoids, leaving the inspector unexpectedly alone, without even having been given the opportunity to demand that Sir Jolyon request his wife to attend next for interrogation.

Once more, he betook himself to the drawing room, this time looking cautiously round the door, to make sure that there was no Sir Jolyon there waiting to ambush him, and relieved, to find that there wasn't, asked Lady Amanda, who had returned to her guests, now that Porky was on her way home, to accompany him into the hall for a moment, where he cravenly asked her for a list of her guests, so that at least he could address, by name, the person to whom he wanted to speak next.

Re-entering the drawing room, a reluctant Moody behind her, Lady Amanda obligingly borrowed Enid's list, handed it over, and left it to him to make his choice, in front of everyone else. It was sheer bad luck that Lt Col. Aloysius Featherstonehaugh-Armitage was at the top of the list, and Moody's pronunciation of the name, as it was spelled, earned him a round of hearty laughter from his merry little group of suspects, thus further reducing his self-esteem.

By the time he left Belchester Towers that evening with his newly returned PC, Moody was in a steaming fury at the lack of respect that had been shown him during the afternoon. In fact, had there been a broom handy, he'd have grabbed it and swept out of the property in a demonstration of his state of anger and high dudgeon. He was now determined to take it out on his family when he got home, just by way of re-asserting his authority on his world and making himself feel better. He was a man who, if bested, always looked for someone further down the pecking order to kick, to ease his frustration and rebuild his self-esteem.

Chapter Eleven
Plotting

When the police presence had removed itself, Lady Amanda courteously showed out her guests, and promised to call on them all to get the feedback from their tour, if they would be so kind as to let her. No one demurred, and she felt it was best to leave this part of what she had wanted to achieve for another day, especially as she felt so excited about being involved with another murder, and was doing her damndest not to show it.

Once back in the drawing room with a cocktail apiece, she began to show the true colours of her mood. 'We're in business again, Hugo! We've got a new investigation, and we've really got a head start on Moody, because we know the world these people move in. We're going detecting tomorrow and I can hardly wait! What say you, old thing?'

'Oh no!' exclaimed Hugo, who had forgotten her comment about the mysterious Virginia and Santa Claus, dismissing it as just a throw-away line, and had hoped she could keep her nose out of police affairs this time. If Moody went digging about in the past for motives, Manda's family had quite a lot of closets absolutely bursting with skeletons.

'Oh, yes, Hugo! I'll bet my shirt that it was something to do with that blasted book he's said to have been writing. If he's going to blow the lid on the County Set, no wonder someone had it in for him. He was just a social climber, after all's said and done. That's the only reason he married Porky when no one else would have her.'

'But, Manda, if he's been poking and prying into

everyone's past, has it not crossed your mind that you'll be a really prominent suspect?'

'What are you talking about, Hugo?'

Lowering his voice, Hugo hissed, 'One: your mother not being dead, two: her running a knocking-shop here for the GIs in the war, three: your daddy's trade on the Black Market, and four: his arms deals after hostilities had ceased.' This statement of facts was greeted with quite a long silence.

'Bum!' said Lady Amanda. 'I hadn't thought about any of that. But that's even more reason for us to get at the truth before Moody. If we can provide him with a murderer, maybe we can get Porky to suppress the book, or take it out of the publisher's hands or something. What you've just said makes it even more urgent that we get on to this murderer's trail before the police. It's not just me that will be in deep doo-doos, it's all my friends as well, and you can bet that their families aren't all sea-green incorruptible.

'We've got to solve this to save the family honour, not only of the Golightlys, of all our friends, Hugo. Don't you see that? It's imperative that we beat that ratty little muff-ball to the solution, for all our sakes. And don't get all holier-than-thou about your own kin. Daddy used to tell stories about your father that would make your hair stand on end.'

'What stories?' Hugo was horrified at the very suggestion that his father had not been the honourable man he remembered and had so much admired and loved.

'You'll have to wait until all this is solved. If keeping you in the dark is the only way I can ensure your help, then keep you in the dark I shall,' said Lady A, with a wicked little smile with which anyone who has ever been emotionally blackmailed would be familiar.

'And what about your lot, Manda?' asked Hugo, a twinkle of triumph in his eyes.

'My lot? What have I got to hide? Apart from what you've already pointed out,' she added, looking rather shame-faced at the embarrassment of riches that Hugo had just listed.

'Surely you haven't forgotten so soon the main reason you used to send your mother back to her apartment in Monte Carlo? What a great potential for current scandal instead of old news: that fatal car crash, after which they buried a woman who wasn't dead, under an erroneous name, while the real Lady E made off to foreign climes, to live out the rest of her years under a false name,' Hugo reminded her. If she could use this fact to send her mother scuttling off back to the continent, then someone else could get considerable mileage out of it in a sensational tell-all book.

'Oh my giddy aunt! None of those things entered my mind, so used to them was I, as part of my own family history. If he breathes a word, not only will the family name be ruined, but Mummy will be extradited and tried for faking her own death, and no doubt there'll be something they can prosecute me for, for using a title to which I'm not entitled, even though I didn't know she wasn't dead. And as for the shares in the family pharmaceutical company – we'll be wiped off the stock exchange.

'Bum!' She declared this last word again with enormous feeling, then followed it with, 'Double bum!' After a few minutes with her chin in one hand, hand balanced on her knee, she looked at Hugo with enormous frightened eyes and intoned soulfully, 'What am I going to *do*, Hugo? They're sure to suspect *me* as it was in *my* house that the murder was committed.'

'Well, I suppose we'll just have to take on the case and expose the real murderer before that chap Moody has time to uncover what old Popeye had included in his book,' replied Hugo, with a long-suffering face.

'Did you say "we", Hugo? Are you really prepared to help me on this one?' she asked, hope dawning on her face.

'Well, I suppose I'd better, old thing, if those stories about my father were as hair-raising as you seem to think they are. Anyway, these people are our friends, and we don't want their reputations to go down the plug-hole just because old Popeye fancied making a bob or two, do we?'

'He never really fitted in, did he? I mean, Porky didn't marry until she was absolutely the last thing left on the shelf, and she didn't exactly do herself proud. He was only a captain, and then insisted that he use the rank socially. I rather thought, at the time, that that was a bit beyond the pale.'

'Me too, Manda! He's not what my papa would have called a pukkah sahib. There's definitely a whiff of the common about him, and I, for one, was never comfortable in his company. He always seemed to be trying to worm information out of one, about one's finances and connections. Definitely not cricket, if you ask me!'

'And he wormed his way into invitations to things to which nobody would normally have dreamed of inviting him. Dolly Pargeter got waylaid by him at some cocktail party or other, she was telling me in the spring, when she suddenly realised he'd smarmed her into inviting him to her spring ball. That wouldn't have been so bad, but when he did turn up, he wasn't wearing white tie, as had been specified, and then he tried to borrow fifty quid from the butler.'

'Shocking! How did Porky put up with him?' barked Hugo, getting quite het-up about these reports of insupportable behaviour on the part of the corpse, then added, 'I suppose we're acting like insufferable snobs, discussing him like this.'

'That's why people like us were put on this earth, Hugo: to be superior. Porky, though, never was a very bright old thing, I suppose. As long as he kept the compliments flowing, she probably just turned a blind eye to his social indiscretions and faux pas, glad to have a man on her arm at long last.'

'So how are we going to go about our investigation, Manda? Have you had any bright ideas?' Hugo wasn't great in the bright ideas department, and usually left all that to someone else with a quicker intellect than his.

'It's so obvious, it's staring us right in the face, Chummy, old stick,' she declared, bounding upright and beginning to pace the room, lost in thought, as the plan developed in her brain.

'It might be to you, but I'm afraid I haven't the faintest idea what it is you plan to do.'

'We visit them all, one by one, and do as much subtle questioning as we can. We never did get to the bit about feedback from my tour, and I think I've a right, having fed them a top-notch afternoon tea, to expect something back in repayment. We'll just call round like I threatened to do, and do some pumping, while we're finding out how they enjoyed their time here.'

'Do you really think we'll get anywhere? If that book of Popeye's is full of stuff that they've been keeping quiet, surely a little discreet questioning isn't going to get them to spill their guts to us?'

'Oh, Hugo, how you are getting into the role! But you're perfectly right. You and I are a good team, but we mustn't forget that we have two other members on our strength. I'm going to send Enid undercover again, and I think I have a role for Beauchamp as well. And don't forget, they're much more likely to confide in us than they would have been to tell all to old Popeye.'

'If they want to have anything to do with it, considering what happened during their tour.' Hugo was highly dubious about their consent to participate in a little feedback session.

It was nearly midnight at the end of a very long Boxing Day, and as Hugo and Lady A sat in the drawing room where Enid had finally joined them, Beauchamp came in with four cocktails on a silver tray, although there were five glasses. He had deemed it socially acceptable that he join in the final discussion of the day, as he had been responsible for so much of its content, murder excepted.

Hugo had his game leg up on a footstool, so that he could rest the knee that had been giving him so much trouble over the last few weeks. Enid was just finishing off her tale of what she had seen and heard that day.

'Ah, Beauchamp, splendid! Just pop the tray on the credenza for a moment will you? I've been waiting for all four of us to be together, for I have something to ask both of you. Hugo and I have been discussing what to do about today's unfortunate event, and have decided that it is our social and moral duty to investigate.

'Both of you were involved in our last investigation, and I would like to ask if I may count on your support for a second outing of the Famous Four? What about it, eh?'

'Will I have to be undercover again, a spy, like last time?' asked Enid.

'Will you be putting yourself in physical danger again, my lady?' asked Beauchamp.

'Hmm. How shall I put this? Yes to your question, Enid, and probably, to yours, Beauchamp.

'Yes, please,' squeaked Enid Tweedie, her eyes sparkling at the thought of her life being elevated above the humdrum for a second time.

'Provided we can miss out the bit where I get knocked on the head and tied to a chair, with sticky tape across my mouth, you can count me in, too,' agreed Beauchamp, in his haughtiest voice.

'Bungo-ho!' cried Hugo, unable to believe that they wanted to play private detectives again with Lady Amanda, and clapped his hands in his enthusiasm.

'So, what drinks have you brought us, to end such an unexpectedly eventful day, Beauchamp?'

The manservant retrieved his tray and, starting with Lady Amanda, began to offload his cargo of colourful glasses. 'A White Christmas for you, my lady: a Wobbly Knee again, for Mr Hugo: and for Mrs Tweedie ...'

'Do call me Enid.'

'How kind. Thank you. For Enid, a Waste of Time – you get two glasses with this, my dear, and their contents might explain the cocktail's name; and a Hopeless Case, for myself.'

'Are you being facetious, Beauchamp?' asked Lady Amanda, as the last two drinks were named and distributed.

'I wouldn't know how to, my lady,' he replied, with the ghost of a twinkle in his eye.

'Before draining her glass in one swallow, Lady Amanda held it aloft and proposed a toast. 'To the Belchester Towers Irregulars! And bugger Baker Street!'

'And then I really must be off, if you would be so kind as to allow Beauchamp to escort me home in the Rolls,' added Enid, totally pricking the balloon of Lady A's mood, with her down-to-earth practicality.

Chapter Twelve
The Belchester Towers Irregulars Strut their Funky Stuff

Hugo awoke at nine o'clock the next morning, because the sound of a human voice, apparently in endless monologue, had insinuated itself into his dream and was drowning out what Carmen Miranda had been trying to whisper in his ear. He would have been quite happy to let things be, but her mangoes were bobbing about on his head to a tango rhythm, and he yielded, eventually, to the inevitable separation from such a lovely scenario, and woke up.

The voice, however, continued, and proved to be coming from the hall, where Lady Amanda was just coming to the end of a telephone marathon in pursuit of the naked truth (and some feedback on her tour).

Pulling on his comfy old dressing gown and stepping into his slippers, he went out into the corridor and walked down to where the instrument lived, only to find her in the action of hanging up for the final time. 'Whatever have you been doing?' he asked, still chagrined about his loss of Carmen Miranda, even if she had assaulted him with her mangoes, 'Filling in for the speaking clock?' His white hair stood up in stiff meringue peaks, and his unshaven face gave him a slightly sleazy look that Carmen Miranda would probably have loved.

'I've been arranging our covert interrogations,' she answered brightly, as if she had been up for hours, which she had, but had not dared to use the instrument until eight o'clock when, even if the object of her call was still dead to the world, a member of staff would be available to note down the time of her visit, and her excuse for paying a call – spurious now of course, as there was something much more enticing afoot.

'I've spoken to Dr Andrew, in the strictest confidence, of course, and he confirmed exactly what I hoped he might: that Porky shouldn't be left alone at the moment, because of the shock she has suffered. I, of course, offered Enid as a live-in nurse for her, until she is feeling herself again, at no cost whatsoever to Porky, as a sort of apology for her husband being murdered under my roof.

'I left him to put the proposal to her, giving him my permission to say that it was all his idea, and then phoned Enid to get her ready to go to work.'

'But I thought she had a live-in maid.'

'Gone to daily, I'm afraid, and refuses to stay overnight any more.'

'How you do wrap people around your little finger. I simply don't know how you do it. Is it because you charm them? Because they're terrified of you? Or are you really a witch?'

'Don't be silly, Hugo. It's because they trust and respect me. Now, where was I? Oh, yes: I've made appointments for one of us to call at some of the households, to talk to them about yesterday, including Porky's.'

'Hey, that's a bit like asking Mrs Lincoln how, apart from the assassination of her husband, she enjoyed the play!' Hugo looked scandalised for a moment.

'Don't be such an old woman, Hugo. It's got to be done. Now, hurry off and get dressed, and get some breakfast down you, so that we can get on with the investigation.'

'What else have you done? I can see something in your eyes that you're not telling me.'

'I've sent Beauchamp out on a little errand, that's all.' Lady Amanda was at her most dangerous when she was playing the innocent.

'And what little errand would that be, then?' Hugo knew her too well.

'I've just asked him to ask a few people a couple of questions.'

'What people and what questions?' Hugo was not going to be fobbed off on this one.

'I've sort of decided, maybe, to have a servants' ball here in the great hall, and I've sent Beauchamp out to question one or two domestic staff as to what they would like to do and to eat at the event. Although, of course, I might not be able to manage it this year, at all.'

'You've sent him round to all the houses of yesterday's guests, to pump their staff, haven't you?'

'I might have.'

'Manda, you are just about the end. I'd hate to be on your hit list: I wouldn't stand a chance,' with which opinion, Hugo toddled off to the dining room, limping slightly, in search of sustenance with which to break his fast.

Luckily, there had been a bit of a thaw overnight, so that Enid Tweedie was able to accomplish her mission of getting to Porky's residence on her bicycle, without the necessity of Beauchamp having to collect and deliver her in the Rolls – which was just as well, as that gentleman had been sent about other business. Her pump primed with instructions, she rang the doorbell of Journey's End at ten o'clock exactly, dressed in what she considered a lady's companion/nurse should wear.

Her sensible tweed coat covered a white blouse with no frills or fussy bits, and a comfortable old tweed skirt that looked as though it had been inhabited by several governesses or nannies in the past. On her feet were sensible lace-up shoes, and her head was protected from the wind by a headscarf which friends had assured her looked very like one that the Queen had worn when filmed out and about at Balmoral.

Her sensible large black handbag held a roll of freezer bags with which to protect any evidence she should find it necessary to 'acquire', and a notebook and several pens (in case one ran out) with which to make notes, during her stay. Enid's overnight bag would be delivered later, when Beauchamp was once again free to carry out this task, as she could hardly have managed the cycle with a suitcase in the wicker basket on her handlebars.

The door was answered by Mrs Twigger, a rotund figure with her hair rolled up underneath a (rather inferior, Enid thought) headscarf, and a button-up overall, for she was just a daily, now, and only worked three hours a day.

'Cor! Am I glad you've got 'ere!' Mrs Twigger exclaimed, looking at Enid as if she were the Archangel Gabriel himself. 'She's in a right old state. I can't do anything with 'er, and I'm not even supposed to be 'ere today. Supposed to 'ave a week orf, I am, and 'ere's me, only two days in me own 'ome, and 'ere I am again. Well, it's not good enough. If I 'adn't known you was comin', I'd 'ave given me notice in there and then, when I got 'ere, what with 'er weepin' an' wailin' all over the place.'

'Never fear! I am here to take the load off your shoulders,' announced Enid, in what she thought of as a confident and trustworthy voice. 'You may go as soon as I've had a word with you about Mrs Barrington-Blyss. I understand she's suffering from severe shock, and I'd like to know everything that's happened since you arrived, so that I can assess what treatment is needed.' Enid Tweedie would never have used the word 'bullshit', but she sure knew how to utilise it.

'I'll tell you what: I'll make us a nice cuppa, and we can sit in the kitchen for a bit, and I'll give you the whole story. What a ghastly thing to 'appen when yer out visitin'.'

Enid trotted into the house and followed the ample behind of the 'daily', with great hopes of what she would find out.

Beauchamp, meanwhile, was sitting at the huge kitchen table at The Manor, the residence of Sir Jolyon and Lady Felicity *ff*olliat DeWinter, being treated like minor royalty. He had a very charming way to him, when given the chance, and he'd certainly done a number on the female staff of the house. They buzzed round him like flies, offering him more tea or another slice of cake, checking to see if his chair was comfortable enough, or would he, perhaps, like another cushion?

One can only state that the manservant, who spent most of his time at the beck and call of Lady Amanda, was in his element. If he couldn't get any sniff of a suppressed scandal from these eager females, then his name wasn't Beauchamp! And he had brought tidings of a possible free knees-up. How popular could a man get?

Although it was nice to be treated like a lord, it wasn't until he was issued with an invitation into the butler's private sitting room that anything in the nature of scandal was to come to light.

Fustion, who had once been valet to The Manor's late master, and had seen the staff of the establishment dwindle until he was the only indoor manservant left, had leaned forward in his chair with a very malicious gleam in his eye, when Beauchamp mentioned the suspicious death at Belchester Towers the day before.

Lifting his right index finger, with which to either conduct or punctuate what he was about to say, he launched into his exact feelings about the deceased. 'That man was an absolute cad. How he ever managed to deceive dear Miss Lesley into marrying him, I will never know.

'He might have fooled some people, but he never

123

fooled me. A gold-digger and a social climber he was, and it looks like he got his just desserts. Always sniffing around, he was, for any little snippet of gossip he could pick up. I heard he was writing a book about the county folks hereabouts, and that it was to be a right nasty one.

'Miss Lesley was a lovely girl in her youth, if you didn't mind a nice roundness to the figure. I've always liked plump women, myself, but she had a real down on her figure, and then found she couldn't stick to no diet sheet for more than a day or two. Many's the time, during a party or a ball here, I've found her sitting all alone in some dark corner, just feeding her face and looking miserable.

'I used to tell her that the right chap would come along one day and sweep her off her feet, but I never thought it'd be that bounder Barrington-Blyss. Right wrong 'un he was. I could tell from the word go. And she was never what you'd call happy. Still went on stuffing her face with anything she could lay her hands on. If she'd met the right chap that would never have been the case.'

'I did hear he'd got a publishing deal, and that his book was due out soon. Just between you, me and the gatepost, do you suppose there's anything about your household in it?' Beauchamp had worded his question carefully, using language that would cunningly persuade Fustion that he was of paramount importance in the *ff*olliat DeWinter household, and it worked.

'I don't know as there's anything that could be proved or not, but there was some sort of monkey business going on when Sir Jolyon's father – the late master, as it were – died – that, I do know for a fact, for it's had me puzzled ever since.'

At this, Beauchamp pricked up his ears and, trying not to look too eager, he leant forward in his chair and encouraged Fustion with a mildly curious look, hoping that he would spill the beans in an effort to appear all-knowing.

'I was valeting the old gentleman at the time, you understand, this place having a much bigger staff. The old master had terrible trouble with his breathing towards the end, probably because he was never to be seen without a cigar sticking out of the side of his mouth.

'Anyway, he eventually took to his bed one winter: didn't even have the puff to go up and down the stairs but, being a cantankerous old bug ... soul, he sent me downstairs when he'd been in bed about a week, saying that he felt well enough to have a little puff, and asking me to fetch him his cigar case from his desk drawer in his study.

'It simply wasn't my case to argue, so off I went, trotting down to the ground floor to fetch him his dratted cigars, but when I got close to the study door, I realised it was ajar, and there was someone on the telephone inside the room. Well, I knew my place, same as everybody else in this household did, so I stopped, waiting for the call to finish, as anyone would've done, if they'd had any manners at all.'

Beauchamp recognised this for what it was: an invitation for him to sanction something that was nothing more nor less than out-and-out eavesdropping. 'That must have left you in a very difficult position, Fustion. If you walked away, whoever it was would have heard you, and you couldn't just walk in on a private telephone call without seeming terribly rude.'

'Exactly, Mr Beauchamp. So I thought the best thing to do would be to stand my ground, wait for whoever it was to finish the call, then tap gently on the door as the call ended; which is exactly what I did do.' The bait had been enticingly dangled again.

'So, who was it, making telephone calls from your late master's study?' Beauchamp was taking the softly-softly approach.

'It was the present Sir Jolyon, Mr Beauchamp, and

what I heard – completely reluctantly, you understand – was a man pleading for more time to clear his gambling debts.'

'No! I had no idea Sir Jolyon was a gambling man.' Lady Amanda would have been proud of her manservant. He was reeling in his fish with enormous skill and dexterity.

'He isn't any more, I can tell you; but back then he was going through a bad time, and was heavily into cards, not to mention debt. He sounded desperate on the telephone, and was begging to be given just a few more days to get the money together.'

'And?' enquired Beauchamp, looking eagerly at the older man, who looked just as keen to tell his story as Beauchamp was to hear it.

'And, I didn't think anything more about it at the time, but the next morning, when I went up to the master to set about washing and shaving him, I was to get the surprise of my life. The maid had been in with his early morning tea, but she'd said he was still asleep, so she'd just left it on the side; he had a foul temper if woken, and she didn't want to catch the rough side of his tongue so early in the morning. He could be a right tartar at times.

'I went up about fifteen minutes later and drew the curtains, and when I turned to wake the old man, I got the shock of my life. There was nothing on this earth that would ever wake my master again, except for, perhaps, the last trump. He was stone cold dead. I can tell you, I nearly passed out cold when I saw him lying there, with no more breaths left to draw. He'd had his last cigar, and I think I rather imagined that that had sent him off to the other side, and I felt so responsible; as if I'd killed him myself.'

'How ghastly for you, Fustion. You must have been riddled with guilt,' interjected Beauchamp, just to keep the story flowing, for he was certain that it hadn't, yet, reached its conclusion.

'I hardly knew what to do next, and I went into what I think is called a sort of auto-pilot mode. I tidied the bed sheets, thinking that he hadn't gone as peacefully as I'd have liked, They were in a fair old mess, as if he'd tossed and turned half the night. I also picked up a pillow from the floor, never thinking how it might have got there, except through his restlessness. I remember standing and staring at it, as if it might hold the solution to my problem of how to inform the household of what had occurred, and the only thing I recall, is looking at the material and thinking the old fellow must have dribbled a lot in the night, for there were quite a few saliva stains on it.'

'Go on,' Beauchamp encouraged him.

'Well, I put the pillow back on the bed, and took myself off downstairs to inform the new master and his wife, who were early risers, and would be at breakfast by now. I'd had such a shock, that I was very conscious of the fact that I would upset their meal, but I had no choice, and went straight in to them. That was when I felt they weren't acting quite right, but I don't really know how to explain it.

'She already looked as if she'd been crying, which I thought rather odd, as they weren't a quarrelsome couple, and when I entered the room, Sir Jolyon jumped up, as if someone had pulled a gun on him. His eyes were round and fearful, and yet I hadn't said a word to them about what had happened.'

'That is odd. Almost as if they already knew, you mean?'

'That's precisely it, Mr Beauchamp, and when I finally did blurt out my news, it had very little effect on either of them. To my mind, they acted very uncharacteristically. On the way down the stairs, you see, I'd already played out the scene in my mind.

'Sir Jolyon isn't a man to use two words when twenty will do, and I thought he'd go off into a right old rant about how the old man didn't deserve to go, and would still be here now if he'd followed medical advice, instead of being bloody-minded and doing exactly as he pleased, blaming me for getting him that last cigar without consulting him. I thought Lady Felicity would burst into tears and have a hysterical turn, weeping and wailing that she never had time to say goodbye properly, and now it was too late.'

'And they did nothing of the sort?'

'You're right about that, Beauchamp. Sir Jolyon himself just blustered something like, 'the old man had to go sometime' and perhaps I would sort out the undertaker, as the doctor had been in recent attendance. Lady Felicity merely said what a relief it was to know that he was no longer suffering, and then I was dismissed.'

'Didn't it play on your mind that something was out of kilter, Fustion?'

'It wasn't my place to say anything. I could've lost my position, and it wasn't really any of my business. I dismissed it from my mind, until that gentleman, who is no gentleman, came snooping around here a few months ago, asking impertinent questions and generally upsetting the staff.'

'I'm assuming you're referring to Barrington-Blyss?' Beauchamp wanted all the 'i's dotted and all the 't's crossed, and would chance to presume nothing.

'That's the feller. Got himself knocked off at your place, yesterday, I hear. Can't say as he'll be missed. From what I've heard. I never could put up with him, as I've already made clear. He was never what you'd call a popular man – more someone who was tolerated because of who he'd married, if you get my drift.'

'Oh, I do, indeed, Fustion. Least said, soonest mended, eh?'

'That's it in a nutshell, Mr Beauchamp. Now, would you like any more refreshments?'

'I have had an adequate sufficiency, thank you. My compliments to the cook on her baking, and I must take my leave now. Thank you so much for sparing the time to talk to me.'

'Is your old gal playing detective again?' asked Fustion as Beauchamp rose from his chair.

'I shall tell her ladyship that you asked after her,' he replied, and winked at the old keeper of secrets at The Manor. They were two of a kind, and they both recognised this fact.

After morning coffee, Hugo had been surprised and delighted to find out that he would be responsible for a fact-finding mission on his own, and not under the beady eye of Lady Amanda.

'Hugo,' she trilled, as he set his empty cup back in its saucer. I want you to go out on reconnaissance for me, this morning.'

'You'll be coming too, though, won't you?'

'No. This is a mission strictly for you. I want you to go over to the Heyhoe-Caramacs' and ask if it's possible to speak to their gardener. His name's Grundle, I believe.'

'What's gardening got to do with the murder?' asked Hugo, perplexed at this request.

'If I remember correctly, he was Col. Henry's father's man, when the colonel was in the army. He must know an awful lot about the old fellow and the household's history, right up to date. If there's anyone at that house who can give us a pointer or two in the right direction, it's Grundle. He's a bit of a grumpy old curmudgeon, but I'll give you a bottle of whisky to take with you as a peace-offering.'

'What shall I tell him I'm there for? I can't just turn up without a reason,' Hugo asked plaintively.

'Tell him I want him to do me some cuttings from all his honeysuckles and clematis. I've complimented him on his climbers in the past, so he'll have no reason to doubt the veracity of the request.'

'Righty-ho, Manda. Where do they live?'

'At a place called The Grange. It's only a few hundred yards up the Belchester Road, so you might as well take the tricycle.'

'In this weather?'

'Hugo, a man has lost his life, and you complain about getting a bit chilly? What are you, a man or a mouse?'

'Squeak,' was Hugo's inevitable answer, but Lady Amanda informed him that Beauchamp had taken the Rolls and would not be back until it was time to prepare luncheon. With that, she bundled him into the hall, handed him his top coat, his hat and gloves, and offered a long stripy scarf to protect his face against the wind. Then, when she had him suitably bundled up, like a rather colourful Egyptian mummy, she whizzed off to the stables and rode the motorised trike round to the front of the house, and helped him on to it. She had left it running, and her last act in seeing him off was to release the brake, giving him a rather unexpectedly wobbly start to his first mission for the day.

Hugo sputtered haphazardly down the drive, muttering insults into the wool of his scarf, containing words such as 'dictator', 'control-freak', and 'blasted Little Miss Bossy-Boots'.

The road had been cleared, so he had little difficulty with snow or ice, and he eventually found it quite revivifying to be puttering along in the bright sunshine under a powder-blue sky, on such a crisp and beautiful day. His spirits rose as he rode, and by the time he'd reached The Grange, he was in a fine mood.

Stopping only to open the gate to admit himself and his machine, he turned the handle-bars towards the greenhouse, in which he could detect a fine clouding of smoke; a sure sign that the old man was in there with his pipe going full blast. Hugo had met him once before, but only in passing, but was sure he could hold his own, on this mission. He liked people and, in general, they like him. It might not be such a bad morning after all.

Meanwhile, shortly after Hugo's reluctant departure, Lady Amanda had been surprised to receive a visitor in the guise of PC Glenister, who stood on the front step and twinkled at her. 'Morning, ma'am,' he greeted her, and gave her a dazzling smile with just a hint of conspiracy in it. 'I thought I'd pop round and keep you up to date with events relating to yesterday's suspicious death.'

'That's very kind of you, young man, er, Constable. Do, please, come in and warm yourself. Tell me, has Inspector Moody sent you?"

'Absolutely not, ma'am. I just thought you'd like to be kept abreast of what the police have turned up.'

'Are you conspiring with me, Constable?'

'Oh, absolutely, ma'am. I saw that look in your eyes yesterday and, as I'd rather get the case wrapped up before New Year when I'm off to visit my family, I thought I'd back you as the winning horse.'

'How very charming and astute of you. So you're proposing to be my police mole, is that it?'

PC Glenister squeezed his eyes nearly shut and made vague clawing motions with his fingers.

'Jolly good impression. Perhaps it might be more comfortable for us, if we're to collaborate, if I called you something less formal than PC Glenister. What is your Christian name?'

'I believe the politically correct expression now is "forename",' he informed her, as a corner of his mouth twitched.

This was a test, she felt, and replied, 'Christian name was good enough for my parents, and it's always been good enough for me, so I repeat, what is your Christian name, PC Glenister?'

'Call me Adrian, ma'am.'

'And you may call me Lady Amanda. Now, what have you got for me? Has old Mouldy-Wump got anything to go on yet?'

'I'm very much afraid he has. That's why I'm here, really. I couldn't bear to see him steal a march on you. Oh, and if anyone should ever find me here when we're consulting, I wonder if you'd be so good as to say that I'm just here on some routine follow-up questions.'

'Excellent idea!' Lady Amanda agreed. 'Now, what's the old windbag got?'

'I'm sorry to have to tell you that he obtained a search warrant this morning, for the deceased's house, having got wind of a book he was writing, that might leave a number of members of the County Set right in the proverbial poo,' he informed her.

'Damn!' swore Lady Amanda. 'And did he find it?'

'I'm afraid so, and there's no point in asking me if I can get access to it, because he's got it locked up in the evidence room with instructions that no one's allowed to retrieve it except himself. That is, he found a paper copy, and confiscated the deceased's computer.'

'Blasted dog-in-a-manger!'

'Exactly! That was the final straw that made me decide to throw my lot in with yours. I think I've got him pretty well summed up now, and I don't want to be working on this case until I draw my pension.'

'Good lad! Stick with Auntie Amanda, and you won't go far wrong. Now, has the book got him any further forward?'

'He was reading it when I left the station, and making some very excited noises. I've got a nasty feeling that he's got his hands on the goods, but he's bound to bungle it somehow. From what I've seen of him, he couldn't detect the location of his own backside with both hands and a mirror. And by the way, there were absolutely no fingerprints to be found on any of the weapons. I thought you'd be pleased to hear that, so at least he's got nothing to go on in that department.'

'Okay, Adrian. You've been up-front with me. I'll now be up-front with you. I've managed to get one of my friends – not a classy one, you understand, just to make that clear – installed in the widow's house as a companion/nurse while she's coming to terms with the shock. So, I've now got someone on the inside, and I intend to use her.'

'Nice one, Lady Amanda. You've stolen a march on him there. He hasn't even thought of putting a WPC in the property, in case Mrs Barrington-Blyss's life is in danger as well.'

'Well, if he does, she'll have good old Enid Tweedie to contend with, and I hear she's pretty good with a loaded handbag.'

Back at the greenhouse, in the gardens of The Grange, Hugo was perched on an old tea chest, drinking whisky-laden tea strong enough to flatten a stevedore, and was well into worming his way into Grundle's confidence.

'… and I know he doesn't really like Manda, because she's so much better a shot than he is. He really resents the fact that a woman should be so good with guns.'

'Well, he certainly doesn't take after his father, that's all I can say.'

'His father was a good man with a gun?'

'I'll say! We had a bit of an adventure during the war, and it was his shooting kept us going until we could get ourselves back to Blighty.' Grundle's rheumy eyes were misted with memories, as they gazed back down the long tunnel to his youth.

'We both went over with the British Expeditionary Force, him and me. I was only a private, you understand, and he was the major, so we weren't buddies, or even on a level where we'd even pass the time of day. Then all hell broke loose, and we found ourselves on our own, cut off from our own lads, and surrounded by bloody Jerries.

'I was a gibbering wreck, with what I'd seen on the beaches, but the major shook me back to my senses and told me that if I wanted to live, I'd have to pull myself together, and listen to him. We weren't going to be able to leave northern France with all this hoo-ha going on, so we'd better get ourselves down south a bit more, and see if we could contact the Resistance.

'I was that shocked that I'd have done anything he told me to do, but he played a cool hand. We travelled only at night. We slept under hedges and in barns at off the beaten track farmhouses. We stole eggs and chickens. We foraged for food as best we could, and it took us a while, but we finally got somewhere where we managed to pick up on the local Resistance fighters.

'Stupid, it seems, looking back on it, now. There we were, being so clever and underhand, moving about the countryside by night, then we got busted for having a whispered chat in one of them 'piss-whar' things. Thank God the Froggy who heard us was on our side.

'He bundled us out of that little stink-hole and into the back of a truck, where he covered us in sacks and drove us off God knows where. In the middle of nowhere we were, when he signalled us to get out. He'd taken us to what looked like the middle of a blasted forest, and suddenly we weren't sure whether to trust him or not. I expected him to hand us straight over to the enemy, but he just stood there whistling a little tune, and soon other men began to materialise out of the trees.

'We'd really landed on our feet, and we knew we were in safe hands. They took us off to an old farmhouse with no neighbour within seeing distance, and gave us some old French clothes to wear, putting our uniforms below the floor in a secret compartment, which I could see already had guns in it. Then they put this heavy old sideboard over the stash. If Jerry came visiting, he would go through the whole place, but they'd got so complacent, those dratted Huns, that they weren't going to move the furniture around looking for secret compartments.'

'You sound like you had quite an adventurous time in La Belle France, what?' Hugo commented, seeing the story in his mind's eye, and turning it into the sort of romantic tale that would have scandalised the old gardener, were he able to read Hugo's thoughts.

'Oh, we worked. It was no holiday camp. We had to sleep in the back of the chicken house, and work in the fields during the day, so we didn't stick out, but they fed us well, and after a couple of days, there was a meeting in this little restaurant nearby. Shutters all closed, closed sign on the door and, inside, all oil lamps and candles, and cloak and dagger.

'They had plans to seriously disrupt the Jerries thereabouts, and we were to be a part of it. Life sort of took on a different rhythm then, if you know what I mean. Working on the land was what I was used to, and a bit of a song and dance, getting up Jerry's nose was fine by me.'

'You must have been very brave, both of you. I hope you were well decorated for your efforts for your country in a foreign land.' Hugo was trying to change up a gear to find out if he was on the right track. This must lead back to Col. Henry at some point, but they were still stuck in the war, when the colonel would have been a mere infant.

'To cut a long story short ...'

'Thank God for that,' murmured Hugo under his breath, under the camouflage of nipping at his eye-wateringly alcoholic cup of tea.

'What I couldn't understand was, several times, seeing the major yammering away with them Jerries, out in the forest where no one could see them. I thought he was gathering information for the Resistance lads, so we could make more of a nuisance of ourselves, but he never said nothing about it afterwards, not even to me.

'We must've been there about a month when this started, and, only a few days later, one of our young Frogs was shot as he left the restaurant. The first shot missed, and he made for the barn over the road, and took one in the shoulder there. He managed to get out and hared off down the road as if all the hounds of hell were after him, but Jerry got his aim together, and he put one through his head, that dropped him like a stone.

'They got us out of there the next day, in case we drew unwanted attention, and passed us on to another group travelling north, to see if they could get us back to Blighty somehow; perhaps on a fishing boat, over the Channel.'

'So, did you ask him what he was chatting so earnestly about with the enemy?'

'I did, Mr Hugo. I waited until we were completely on our own, and I put it to him that I'd seen him talking to them, and he said he'd just been passing the time of day in German, to sort of keep his hand in with the language. A couple of days later, just when we were about to try to get back home, we heard through the unit we were now with, that the unit that had looked after us had been carrying out a raid on a railway line, trying to de-rail a Jerry train, when the Jerries appeared out of nowhere, and just fired until they were all dead. Ten men from the little village we were staying near were killed that night, and the Jerries went back there and shot all the males that were left: old men and teenagers, some of them; even kiddies.'

'What did your major have to say about that?' Hugo had half an idea he was on to something here, and ought to stick it out to the bitter end.

'I thought he'd be devastated, like I was. They were people we'd got to know. In fact, if we'd stayed on, we would have been in that raiding party with all the rest of them. But, that was the funny thing: he didn't seem to give a damn. Just said it was part of the price of warfare, and that we should just forget it and get on with what we were posted to do.'

'I say! That was a bit cold of him, wasn't it?' asked Hugo.

'Cold weren't the word for it. We went our separate ways, though, having got back, and I didn't see him again until near the end of the war. We met again in a convalescent home. We'd both got a Blighty shot, and it was the end of our service for that war. He'd taken a hit to the shoulder that had done a lot of damage to the bones, and I was left with a game leg.

'We got talking, one day, and I suppose I was a little down, what with thinking what on earth I was going to do when the show was over. I mean, how much chance does a man with a game leg have against fit candidates, for a physical job? I reckoned I'd end up in the gutter, and that's when he turned up trumps. He gave me his card and said to get in touch with him when I was de-mobbed, and he'd take me on as his gardener. And here I am, still working on the same garden I came back from the war to.'

'Wonderful story, old man. Been most interesting talking to you. I'd better be off, though. I was only sent here to ask you about those cuttings,' Hugo said, his head full of enough food for thought for a cranial banquet.

'Tell her ladyship that, as soon as they've struck, I'll bring them over and hand them over to Beauchamp. He'll know what to do with them. Grand fellow! And give old Grundle's regards to her ladyship. Fine figure of a woman, she is. If I was only a few years younger …' The old man trailed off, a leering smile forming fleetingly on his lips.

Hugo entangled himself with his coat and scarf in an effort to re-don them, and generally made himself ready for the return journey. Old Grundle had to give him a hand with his gloves, as he'd managed to get them on the wrong hands and then stood helplessly, wondering how on earth he could right the situation.

With a final twist of the scarf round his neck, he headed, rather haphazardly, towards the tricycle, mounted it, started the engine, released the brake. And drove straight into the pile of manure that was quietly and warmly steaming in the cold, as it rotted at the end of the garden.

When Lady Amanda opened the doors, slightly later in the afternoon, Hugo entered at a staggering run, turned a full three-hundred-and-sixty degree circle, staggered to his left, and ended up hugging the newel post at the bottom of the stairs, several feet of scarf draped in his wake, like the trail of a giant snail, and his hat down over his eyes at a very jaunty angle. 'H'llo, Manda,' he intoned, joyfully and slowly, taking great care with what enunciation he could muster.

Still on the step, she found Grundle, his hat held respectfully in his hands. 'I'm terribly sorry to bring Mr Hugo back like this, your ladyship, but he seemed to be having a bit of trouble with his old pins.'

'But, how on earth did you get him back here? And where's the tricycle?' Although Lady Amanda cared very much about Hugo's welfare, there was an expensive tricycle in this equation to consider as well. Hugo would, no doubt, be sober in the morning, but a new tricycle cost money.

'Down by my greenhouse, your ladyship. I loaded him into the bucket of the digging machine and drove him here by the back route. My digger's just across there, near the stables. I hope you don't mind.'

'I am most pleased with your ingenuity, Grundle, and I shall tell Col. Henry so, when I see him.'

'Thank you very much, your ladyship. I'll be taking my leave of you then. Good day!'

As Lady Amanda closed the door, she discovered that Beauchamp must have helped Hugo to a more comfortable position, and opened her mouth to locate him. 'Hugo! HUGO! Where the devil are you?'

A groan answered her from the direction of the library, and she turned and headed in that direction. She knew Grundle of old, and Hugo had probably fallen for the offer of a nice cup of tea. Nice cup of tea, be damned! It was nearly neat whisky, the way that old rascal served it.

Well, he'd better be feeling tiptop by the witching hour. She had work planned for them that night, in the wee, small hours, and she didn't want him blundering around giving away what they were up to.

After a late and solitary luncheon, Lady Amanda decided to leave Hugo to sleep off his excesses, for he had, seemingly, dispatched himself to bed in the library, not only without any supper, but without several more meal stops along the day's menu. As 'it' had happened in her residence, she thought she'd pay a courtesy call on Porky, to see how the old thing was doing. If, during that time, she had the opportunity to conspire with Enid, then so much the better. Before she left, she dropped a small brown bottle into her handbag, and smiled to herself. Some people didn't need official search warrants.

When Enid saw who was on the doorstep, her face became a mask of misery. 'Oh, Lady Amanda, I don't know how to break this to you,' she began.

'I know what you're going to say, Enid, but I already know about the police search. Never fear, there's bound to be more than one copy. No one puts all that effort into writing a book and then only keeps one copy of it. There'll be at least one more copy, or an earlier version of it around. The original notes are still probably tucked away somewhere, too. How hard did they search?'

'They were only here a few minutes. They found a manuscript on his computer and took that away with them, saying that the book would probably contain the motive for the captain's murder, and would be stored and given in evidence in any subsequent trial. They also found a copy for proofing in paper and took that as well.'

'How did poor old Porky take it?' They were speaking in whispers, but poor old Porky was obviously aware of their conversation, and her voice called out to Enid plaintively, 'Who's that, Mrs Tweedie? I don't want any visitors at the moment, not while I'm feeling like this.'

Before the lady of the house had time to draw breath, Lady Amanda was bustling into the drawing room, all smiles, pulling a pile of ladies' magazines and a small box of chocolates from her capacious handbag, and asking after the welfare of the recent widow. 'Poor, poor Porky,' she crooned, sitting down beside the woman and asking, 'How are you going to manage without Popeye?'

'I don't know how I shall manage,' Lesley Barrington-Blyss replied. 'Popeye did all the household accounts and managed all the bills and his own business affairs, and I haven't the faintest idea where to start with all that paperwork, let alone arranging a funeral for him. It might have been I who had all the money, but I had nothing whatsoever to do with the handling of it, and now I'm all at sea. I've no idea how to go about managing my own affairs.'

She spoke in a voice that gave the impression of husky grief, but Lady A noticed that her fingers were working on the cellophane round the chocolate box in an effort to get at the contents as she spoke, an independent action that said more about the way she really felt than any words could.

'Let me help you with that, old girl,' offered Lady Amanda, reaching forward, but Porky merely looked down into her lap with surprise. 'I had no idea I was doing that!' she stated. 'It must be one of those automatic reactions that people speak of.'

'I'll just get them open for you and then I'll go. You

need everything from which you can derive comfort at a time like this, as well as a lot of time on your own to reflect on what has evidently caused an enormous upheaval in your life. There you go, my dear. I hope you enjoy them.'

With that, she left the room and sought out Enid in the kitchen, who was forward thinking, and was already making a pot of tea. 'Psst! Enid!' she hissed, opening her bag once more, as Enid poured the amber cascade into three cups. 'I've got something here for you, and I want you to do exactly as I tell you to do with them.'

'What are you scrabbling about looking for?' asked Enid, whispering again, in the conspiratorial way they had spoken in the hall.

'Aha! There it is!' said the older woman, and produced a small brown bottle from her bag, opened it, and placed two tiny white tablets in the palm of Enid's hand. 'Take these, crush them between two spoons, dissolve them in a little water, and then sneak them into anything in which she might not notice a slightly bitter aftertaste.'

'Like what?' Enid had only been there a few hours, and knew nothing of Mrs Barrington-Blyss's daily habits.

'She always has coffee after dinner, and she has it black and strong, with no sugar. Slip it into her coffee, and make sure you manage to get her upstairs as quickly as possible.'

'What on earth are they?'

'Sleeping tablets. And they work like magic. Don't ask any more questions. Just make sure you get her to swallow them,' ordered Lady Amanda.

'Why? I expect the doctor's left something for her anyway.'

'Because, when Hugo and I get here about midnight, we're going to turn this place upside down, looking for another copy of Popeye's book. I don't know what he's put in it, but I can't just see my friends socially ruined. I heard he had been boasting about absolute dynamite, and I don't want it to blow up in the face of anyone I know.'

'But we're sure to get caught,' Enid squeaked, starting to shake.

'How? Even if she wakes up, she will be too dopy to remember anything in the morning, and if there's anyone who can see lights on in the house, they'll know there's been a recent bereavement. That sort of thing sparks all sorts of out of character behaviour, such as roaming around the house at night.'

'I don't like this at all, lady Amanda,' Enid opined, looking anxious.

'I didn't ask you to like it Enid, I asked you to do it. Those are two totally different things. Got it?'

'Got it.'

Back at Belchester Towers, Lady Amanda went straight to her desk, having made sure the doors to the library and her study were shut. Hugo was making a hell of a racket in there, mumbling to himself, snoring and even once breaking into song. She needed to gather her thoughts and make some notes. There was work she knew she would have to conduct on the computer, but she needed to see her thoughts in writing first, so that they would gel in a comprehensible way.

After a moment of contemplation, she began to write. *Same one-shouldered shrug.* Then followed that with *Head on one side when asking a question to which the expected answer is 'no'.* Here, she paused for a moment and mumbled, 'But couples do get very alike when they've been together for a long time. Might be nothing at all.'

She then gnawed on her pen for a couple of minutes, before jotting down, *Auction catalogues – sales during the two years prior to five years ago. Ring Lady Mumbles! Births, marriages and deaths. What is Somerset House called now? Use search engine!*

Lord above, she was thirsty. That tea with Enid had

disappeared without trace. Putting down her pen, she called, 'Beauchaargh!' The man was already behind her. She'd never known a man so cat-like, and was wondering if he led a double life as a cat burglar. His sudden appearances must have taken months, if not years, off her life.

'I didn't want you to wake Mr Hugo,' Beauchamp informed her in a low voice.

'I don't think a cannon would wake him, at the moment. You've had a mug of Grundle's tea before, haven't you?'

'Oh, no! Not the tea!'

'I'm afraid so,' she confirmed.

'Well, what may I get you, my lady?' asked the manservant, at a more normal volume. 'If he actually drank that witches' brew, he'll be out for hours yet.'

'I think I'll take my afternoon tea a little early, if you don't mind, Beauchamp. Then I'm going to do a little more research on the computer, before going to bed for a few hours. I have a little investigation to carry out tonight, and I want to be as alert as possible for it.'

'Very good, my lady,' answered that good man, not batting an eyelid at what his employer had just told him. 'Do you wish me to be in attendance in case there's any, er, bother?'

'I think that might be a very good idea. I don't want to involve you in anything criminal, but we might need to make a quick getaway.'

'How jolly invigorating. I shall look forward to it with enormous anticipation.'

'I somehow thought you would,' replied Lady A, dropping him a half-wink.

After taking her tea, her ladyship spent two hours surfing the net, tutting and expostulating in a genteelly mild way at what she read. Her notepad beside her, she jotted down what she considered important from her searches, then left it to ferment in her subconscious. She wouldn't think about any of this until the morrow, for there were other plans afoot before then.

At six-thirty, she rang for Beauchamp and asked him if he would be so good as to make sandwiches and coffee for eleven o'clock, and to rouse her and Hugo when all was ready. It wasn't a long drive to Journey's End, and they'd have time to assemble some sort of plan for the search.

'I suggest that you awaken Mr Hugo as well, and get him properly settled in his own bed. If we suddenly spring coffee and sandwiches on him, on top of the fact that we're going out to make an illegal entry to one of our friend's houses, he won't be too pleased, if he wakens in the library, wondering what on earth happened to the rest of his day.'

'Very good, my lady,' spake Beauchamp, and went off in the direction of the library on his unenviable mission.

Chapter Thirteen
A Midnight Misadventure

Hugo hadn't just been grumpy when woken from his alcohol-induced sleep in the library; he was pretty tetchy when he was woken again at eleven o'clock, grumbling about madcap schemes and batty old women. He then informed them that he'd been so bucked about by the tricycle and had lain at such an awkward angle while he was sleeping off his 'tea' that he could barely walk, and would have to take his sticks with him or he wouldn't be able to come at all.

'Hugo, how on earth do you think we can go off on this mission with you clumping along with two walking sticks? Are you mad, man?' asked Lady Amanda.

'Take it or leave it. I'd be quite happy to go straight back to bed.'

'Oh, no you don't! I need you there. I need all the eyes we can get, to get this search done, and you don't get out of it that easily. Buck up, man! Where's your sense of adventure?'

'Back in my bed, where I ought to be too,' he replied, poking his tongue out at her, as he had done as a youngster.

'Put that thing away and pull yourself together. You're probably just suffering from low blood sugar, and here's good old Beauchamp with coffee and sandwiches for us. That'll put some lead in your pencil.'

'Should I need to make any notes, I shall use my trusty fountain pen,' replied Hugo in a huffy voice, but he was reaching for a sandwich as he said it. It would be as pointless to try to hold Lady Amanda back as it would be to try to halt the sea in its progress inland, and he, unlike King Canute, knew when he was beaten.

At eleven-thirty, Lady Amanda hooshed him along to get ready to go, as she had arranged for Enid to let them into Journey's End at midnight, a suitable time for an illicit adventure in her opinion, then wished she hadn't, as he appeared wearing so many layers of clothes that his movement was restricted.

'What on earth do you think you're doing, Hugo? What, exactly, are you wearing for this forbidden little outing?'

Hugo looked down at himself and explained totally ingenuously that he had on his usual pullover, over which he had added a quilted button-in lining under his overcoat, a scarf, mittens, and his trilby. 'It is rather late and the weather has been inclement. After what happened this morning, I want to be adequately dressed to cope with the night temperature.'

'But we're going house-breaking! How on earth do you expect to be able to search in silence and move about the house with stealth, when you look like a Michelin man, and with only half the limited mobility you usually have?' asked Lady Amanda in exasperation.

'Don't know,' replied Hugo, not really getting the point at all. 'What on earth do you think you're doing?'

Lady Amanda was, in fact, pulling off Hugo's hat and scarf, and had already started undoing the buttons of his overcoat as he asked his question. 'You're not going out in all those layers. You'll give the game away before we've even got out of the hall, blundering around in half a wardrobe's worth of clothes. There, that's better!'

Hugo was now stripped down to his indoor pullover again. 'But, I don't understand. I thought you told me to get ready. That's all I've done.'

'I asked you to get ready for entering somebody's

146

house without their permission, and giving it a jolly good search. Stand there and wait for me, and I'll get you what you need.'

'Hang on! Can't I at least have my scarf back?'

'Absolutely not!' she called over her shoulder. 'You'd only knock over something with it or, knowing you, trip over it and make a hell of a row.'

Lady Amanda joined him shortly with a navy blue balaclava helmet, hand-knitted by her mother during the war. 'Here you are, Hugo. Put that on. The moth doesn't seem to have got at it,' she instructed him, mirroring his action with the twin of his headgear.

'Now, take these,' she told him, holding out a torch and a pair of horribly pink rubber gloves.'

'What on earth do I need these for?' he asked.

'Well, you don't suppose we can just stroll in and turn lights on willy-nilly, do you? And I don't want you leaving any fingerprints. If it's suspected that the place has been turned over, that ferret-faced Moody will be in there like a shot, looking for traces of whoever it was who had been searching. I don't want him to come sniffing round here because you haven't had the sense to wear gloves.'

'But I look like I'm about to do the washing up, Manda. And I'm going to catch my death without at least a coat on.'

'Firstly, this is not a fashion parade. We're looking for evidence in a case of murder, and secondly, we'll be in the Rolls for most of the journey. I don't know if you've noticed, but it is adequately heated, and I'm sure Porky doesn't keep her house at sub-zero temperatures, even at night. When you're not in one, you'll be in the other, so stop whingeing, and let's get off, or Enid will wonder where we've got to.'

'But surely Porky will hear us.' Hugo thought he had a good point here, as he'd certainly know if someone was rummaging about near his bedroom.

'Not a problem, Hugo. I've got Enid to drug her.' Lady A's face betrayed not a shred of conscience.

'You've done what?' Hugo's mouth was agape at what he'd just heard.

'I just slipped a couple of sleeping tablets to Enid and gave her instructions for administering them. By the time we get there, Porky should be sleeping the sleep of the dead.'

'Manda! That's hardly cricket, is it?' Hugo was appalled.

'No, but then, neither is murdering a man in my home, and I am determined to get to the bottom of it, and see the murderer put behind bars. Popeye may not have been the easiest man to like, but he didn't deserve to be murdered, and that's that! So let's be off! Hugo, what the Christopher Columbus are you doing with those walking sticks?'

'I've been trying to get through to you that my knee's been giving me severe gyp, but you've either not taken it in, or ignored me completely.'

'But you can't go round a house in the middle of the night with two sticks and a torch. How are you going to hold the torch?'

'Don't you worry about that, Manda: I shall sort out how to do it when we get there. It's a bit late now to be worried about the sticks. A little more sympathy and care when I first mentioned it, might have negated the need to use them at all.'

'Hugo Cholmondley-Crichton- Crump, I shall swing for you one of these days. Put your Marigolds in one trouser pocket, the torch in the other, and let's get out of here before dawn breaks and finds us still standing here bickering.'

'Will Beauchamp be coming in with us?' asked Hugo, knowing he was pushing his luck.

'No he certainly will not. He has to stay with the car in case we need to make an emergency get-away. Now get yourself through that door before I lose my temper with you.

At Journey's End, Beauchamp dropped them off at a pedestrian side-entrance, well screened by trees, and switched off the engine. 'Remember,' he said, 'just push the call button on your mobile phone, and I'll start the engine, ready to make a break for it. The phone's already programmed with my number, so all you've got to do is push 'send'.'

'Walk on the grass, Hugo, not on the path,' directed Lady A, remembering that the path was gravel, and walking on it would be the night-time equivalent of having a brass band escort them to the dwelling.

'But the grass is crunchy with frost, and my feet'll get frozen,' Hugo moaned.

You can put them in a mustard bath when we get back,' whispered his companion.

'But I'll get chilblains,' he went on.

'Hugo?'

'Yes, Manda?'

'Would you like a smack in the mouth?'

'No, thank you. I feel I shall be just fine if I walk on the grass, and a mustard bath would be very soothing.'

'Good boy, Hugo!'

There was no need for torches, as the bitterly cold night boasted a clear sky, and moonlight lit their way adequately, and might prove of some use in helping them navigate their way around the house.

'Manda?'

'What now?' Lady Amanda was getting a bit fed up with the peevish note in Hugo's voice.

'My sticks are slipping in the frost.'

'Then take my arm until we get to the front door. Really! It's like taking a five-year-old to the dentist, taking you anywhere.'

'I just don't want a broken hip,' Hugo whispered plaintively.

'You'll get a split lip, if you moan any more. Now, pull yourself together and … oh, my God!' Lady Amanda had abruptly halted and frozen in position, a condition that had nothing whatsoever to do with the cold.

'What is it, Manda?' asked Hugo, his blood suddenly running colder than the outside temperature could possibly be responsible for.

'There's a policeman on guard outside the house. Don't move! We'll have to wait until he does a circuit of the property, before we can give Enid the signal to let us in.'

They stood in silence for exactly two minutes, before Hugo said, with an element of urgency in his voice, 'Manda?'

'What is it this time, Hugo?' she answered, wondering what he was going to complain about next.

'Manda, I need to *go*. Now!'

'Just like a man!' she hissed angrily. 'Out of the house for five minutes, and you need to use the lavatory. Well, you'll just have to hang on until we can get inside, or go behind one of the bushes.'

'I can't 'go' outside. I was very strenuously potty-trained, you know,' he replied, a note of anguish entering his voice.

'Look, he's going!' Lady Amanda cut in. 'The policeman! He's off on a tour round the house, probably to check all the doors and windows. Now's our chance. Run!'

'!'

'Make a noise like an owl, Hugo, like you used to, when we were young. That's our signal to Enid to get the front door open.'

Lady Amanda remembered well the realistic owl hoots that Hugo used to produce, cupping his hands together and blowing expertly through his thumbs but, tonight, his hands stayed firmly at his sides on his sticks. '*Toowit-*

toowoo,' Hugo warbled, giving it his best shot, but sounding more like a lame sound-effect in a very cheap and amateur production.

Lady A stood rooted to the spot with horror, her fond memories scattered by this parody of his old skill. 'What on earth do you think you're playing at?' she hissed, sounding like an angry snake. 'You used to do it with your *hands*, Hugo! I could've *said* 'toowit-toowoo'. You were supposed to blow through your thumbs and make a noise that at least sounded like an owl, and not some old man trying, and clearly failing, to sound like one.'

Still holding firmly to his sticks, Hugo gave a shrug, almost Gallic in its expressiveness. 'I can't do that any more, Manda. Arthritis! My hands just aren't the same shape as they were. Tempus has fugit-ed, and all that, and I can't make a silk purse out of a sow's ear, even for you and for old times' sake. Sorry!'

'Miss Marple never had this sort of trouble!' she retorted, knowing that comparisons with Agatha Christie's heroine would come into play at some part of the investigation. 'Look, Enid must have heard you anyway. She's opening the door. Quick!'

'!' Once again, Hugo was speechless at her hopeless command. The only 'quick' he could manage was being alive, and when he stopped being able to do that any more, he would be so slow, he would be dead.

At the door, Enid was hopping up and down with nerves, and scooped them through the entrance as if she were a human ladle. 'Thank goodness you're here at last,' she said, 'I've been tiptoeing to this door and opening it at the sound of every owl for the last hour. My nerves are shredded, because, every time I came to open it, there was that PC Glenister.

'My heart was in my mouth, I can tell you, but each time, he just bade me a polite 'good evening', smiled and touched his helmet in greeting, as if it were nothing out of the ordinary for an elderly woman to be running to the front door every five minutes, at this time of night. I felt I should die of embarrassment after the last time, for I'm almost sure I heard him say, 'They'll be here soon.' But at least, thank God, I knew *that* one was Mr Hugo's,' she concluded with relief, only to have her complaint cut short by Hugo's urgent whispering.

'Where's the lavatory? Tell me quickly! Cold weather always does this to me,' he explained, shooting a look full of daggers at his partner in crime. 'Urine contains DNA – even I know that – and I don't want us to be arrested because of the presence of my 'doings' on the hall carpet!'

As Hugo unburdened himself (as quietly as possible, to avoid any one of them suffering unnecessary embarrassment – oh! how he missed the bees or the flowers on the old Victorian lavatory pans, which at least gave a man something to aim at) in a small cubicle just off the hall, Lady Amanda explained, as if to a child, why Enid had been wasting her time for the last fruitless sixty minutes. 'My dear woman, to arrive early is as bad-mannered as to arrive late so, of course, we're here at the exact hour. What else did you expect of us?'

Ignoring this finer point of etiquette, so as to waste no more time, Enid explained that she'd done exactly as she'd been asked, and administered the drug in a cup of cocoa, which Porky, unexpectedly for her, took without sugar. 'She didn't notice a thing, then said she felt absolutely exhausted, and I helped her up to bed. That was about three hours ago, but I don't know how long the tablets will work for.'

'Why did you give them to her so early?' asked Lady Amanda, frowning crossly. She'd hoped that they would be slipped to her about eleven o'clock.

'Because I always go to bed at about half-past nine,' replied Enid, without a thought to her lack of logic.

'You blasted idiot, Enid. You knew you were going to

let us in at midnight, so why didn't you wait a couple of hours?'

Enid's hands flew to her mouth. 'Oh, Lady Amanda, I just didn't think. I could have stayed up later, couldn't I?'

'Of course, you blithering idiot, but we must just make the best of things. You're going to have to be on guard on the landing now, in case she wakes and tries to leave her bedroom. Take a glass of water up with you, then you've got an excuse to be out of your room. You can either say you went to get it for yourself, or you went to get it for her, but, whatever you do, don't let her come out of her room.'

'Of course. Of course. Anything you say. I'm *so* sorry.'

'First things first,' said Lady A, ignoring her apologies. 'Where's Popeye's study?'

'Upstairs in the box-room,' Enid informed them, steeling herself for Lady Amanda's reaction to this unhappy news.

'Upstairs? God deliver me!' She sighed deeply, as if the world were full of fools, and she the only sensible one in existence. 'Well, we've no choice. You go up to the landing and keep an eye on her door, and Hugo and I will follow you up to search. We'll just have to play this one by ear. Now, off you go!'

Enid tiptoed up the stairs, her legs trembling with fear and adrenalin. Hugo went next, placing his sticks with care as he slowly climbed. Lady Amanda followed behind – just in case Hugo fell, and she had to catch him.

All went well until Hugo reached the half-landing, when one of his sticks slipped on the wood at the edge of the carpet of the stair he was just mounting. It shot sideways, and he was unable to do anything about it as it hit the dinner gong on the half-landing with a sonorous and echoing 'bong'.

The three of them became a frozen tableau, each arrested mid-action, as if part of a paused film. Amanda was the first to react, hearing movement from Porky's bedroom and a series of short moans. She fled back down the stairs, dragging a bewildered Hugo in her wake, his sticks in one hand, as Enid rushed to the bedroom door to prevent Porky coming out on to the landing to find her house invaded by midnight friends.

Hugo did his best to dismount as rapidly as he could manage, given the state of his joints, and the vigour with which he was being pulled, but was given a jolt of unexpected haste as he heard a key turn in the front door, and a voice call out, 'Is everything all right in there?' The last things he remembered before he was in darkness, were a hearty shove between the shoulder blades and the sound of a door slamming shut behind him.

PC Glenister entered the darkened hallway of Journey's End, having heard the sounding of the gong, and wondering if it was a distress call from one of the ladies inside. 'Is everybody okay?' he called, shining his torch around in an effort to locate whoever had instigated the metallic 'bong'.

'I'm up here,' called Enid, desperate to distract him from looking around too rigorously downstairs. 'Mrs Barrington-Blyss needs putting back to bed. There's nothing to worry about,' she reassured him, keeping the fingers of both hands crossed. 'I'll be down in a minute.'

'I'll just take a quick look around down here then,' he replied, and headed for the drawing room door. Being about his lawful business, he had no hesitation in switching on the light before checking the room and, behind the largest of the sofas, discovered Lady Amanda stretched out flat on the floor, Hugo's sticks, one each side of her, aligned tidily with her body.,

Giving her a smile and a polite wave, he switched off the light and left the room, checking next, the dining room. The most convenient (in more ways than one) door was that of the downstairs lavatory, and, on opening that, he found Hugo standing with his back to him, his hands on the low cistern and his head turned over his shoulder with the most innocent of expressions on his face.

'Not interrupting, am I?' asked the young policeman, in embarrassment.

'Not at all,' replied Hugo. 'I'm just hiding in here.'

'Good idea, sir. Wish I'd thought of it first,' was PC Glenister's somewhat puzzling answer.

At that moment, Enid could be heard tripping down the stairs, her head a whirl of anxiety about being caught red-handed like this. Her look of inquisition at the PC was one that said she was about to face the rest of her life with a criminal record. 'Everything all right?' she croaked, almost cringing away from him as she awaited the arrests that would surely follow.

'Everything's absolutely dandy down here. Got her back to bed?' he enquired, a hopeful expression on his face.

'Sleeping like a baby again,' Enid replied, wondering why events were not unrolling according to the doom-laden script she had written in her head.

'I'll get back outside then,' he informed her, then let a small smile curve his lips. 'If you're looking for the others, you'll find Lady Amanda behind the sofa in the drawing room, and Mr Hugo in the downstairs cloakroom. Very fastidious man, Mr Hugo. Even wears rubber gloves to go to the lavatory, I noticed,' he joked.

Enid ignored this seemingly inexplicable remark, and merely looked relieved. In fact, her whole body slumped as she received the somewhat inexplicable news that he knew the others were there, but planned to do nothing about it. She might not be able to explain his reaction, but she could certainly appreciate it, and saw him out of the door with a feeling of disbelief. They were going to get away with it after all!

Chapter Fourteen
A Bit More Pumping is Required

Breakfast was cancelled the next day at Belchester Towers, as was lunch, and brunch was declared to be the most appropriate meal, after such a late night and all the trauma that it had involved. They had managed to make a search of the house, with Hugo safely tucked away in the drawing room, keeping out from under Lady Amanda's feet. Enid had even been able to join in, but, of a copy of the manuscript, or even notes pertaining to it, they had found no sign, and the night's adventure had not even been discussed in the car back to the Towers.

They all three retired straight to bed after arriving home, an air of dejection about the trio, who had had such high hopes of that night's clandestine activities, so the first chance there was of any discussion, was at the brunch table the next day, and very late in the day, it was, too.

'Why on earth didn't we get carted off in handcuffs last night? We were caught red-handed, in someone else's house, at an un-Godly hour, and we could have been up to anything. That young constable just made the most extraordinary comment, and treated it like it was an everyday thing for him, to find interlopers in strangers' lavatories.'

'He's one of *us*, Hugo,' explained Lady Amanda, with a rather smug smile.

'What do you mean, *one of us*? Are you sure you don't mean *one of them*, breaking in on a man when he's in the lavatory?'

'Were you actually conducting any business, Hugo?

And don't be so bigoted!'

'No, I was just hiding. And I'm not! Bigoted, that is.'

'Well, there you are then. That proves it, doesn't it?'

'Proves what?'

'That he's one of *us*. He came to see me yesterday, you know.'

'When?' asked Hugo, his voice high with indignation that he had not been apprised of this visit.

'When you were off drinking toxic tea with that old devil Grundle.'

'You could still have told me when I got back.' Hugo felt quite huffy about this clandestine visit, and his total lack of knowledge of it.

'Oh, no, I couldn't. If you remember, you spent the afternoon sleeping off your cup of 'tea', snoring like a grampus in the library, until I got Beauchamp to put you to bed.'

'You could've told me when I woke up,' he challenged her.

'Well, I didn't. You were too grumpy. Now, shut up, and let's work out today's plan of action. We've only got the afternoon and evening left, and three other households to infiltrate.'

'At least we won't be sneaking about like thieves in the night again.'

'Thieves in the night do *not* bang gongs with their walking sticks, Hugo.'

'Fair point, Manda. Fair point.'

After a lot of discussion, which necessitated Beauchamp joining them at table, it was decided to split the work up thus: Hugo was to go off into the woods and 'pump' Sir Montacute Fotherington-Flint's gamekeeper, hoping that he wouldn't be off in the family's woods somewhere doing something incomprehensible and gamekeeper-ish.

'As a boy, when he first started there as a boot-boy, he

was a favourite of the housekeeper, so it would be a good idea to see if you can get him reminiscing about when he first came to the house. He, no doubt, picked up endless bits and pieces of household gossip, just because he was so unimportant,' she informed him.

'Beauchamp, I'd like you to just drop in for a chat with Major Mapperley-Minto's man. Old Monty likes a drink or ten, and he can be very confiding when he's in his cups. It will have been his man's duty to make sure he got to bed safely, and many a confidence has been shared after dark with a close member of one's staff, with a bellyful of booze.'

'Very good, my lady, and that's Beecham, if you don't mind,' chanced the manservant.

'It's Beauchamp, or I'm a Chinaman, and I don't speak a word of Mandarin. Now, I, meanwhile,' she swept on, without a second thought for her manservant, who was standing directly behind her, repeatedly mouthing 'Beecham' silently to the back of her head, 'shall pay a polite call on the Featherstonehaugh-Armitages. Stinky and Donkey,' she clarified, as Hugo was not very good at remembering names, which was ironic, considering the clunking great moniker he himself possessed, 'and I have a few other little calls to make, before the afternoon is out. All clear about what you're doing?'

'Yes, Manda,' agreed Hugo, nodding his head in a vague way.

'Yes, my lady,' concurred Beauchamp, and turned to leave the room.

'One moment, Beauchamp. Just a word before you go.'

'Yes, my lady?'

'I presume you had forgotten about the mirror facing where I was sitting, when you were behind me.'

'I had, indeed, my lady,' said Beauchamp. 'Very remiss of me,' he added, turning a nice shade of pink.

'Dis-missed!' The troops were dispatched.

Beauchamp needed no excuse to call at The White House, as he often dropped in to see the valet/butler, Mr Tinker, when he had a half-day free, and was, therefore, welcomed without question, and shown into Tinker's sitting room.

'Hey, there, Beechy! How are you doing?' he was hailed, before he was fully through the door.

'I'm doing fine, Tinker. How are you? I haven't seen you since well before Christmas,' replied Beauchamp, suddenly coming over all 'hail fellow, well met'.

'All the better for seeing your smiling face. Now, what can I do for you, or have you just come over for one of our little chats?'

'On the button, as usual, Tinker. At this time of year I find I get very nostalgic, and I thought, if there's another man in Belchester who would understand how I feel, it's good old Tinker at The White House.' Lady Amanda would not have recognised this Beauchamp.

'I know just what you mean. You get to thinking about all those other Christmases and New Years you've spent in the same place, and it really does get you remembering old times, doesn't it?'

Accepting a tankard of ale, Beauchamp prepared to steer the conversation around to the possibility of dark doings in the household, way back in the past.

Tinker had, to a certain extent, picked up some of his habits from his employer, and it was while he was pouring Beauchamp's second pint, and his own fourth, that he came over all confidential, and told the other a story that he had heard no hint of in any of the other residences of quality in the county.

'My two are getting on a bit, just like yours. Funny the way your old lady just ran into old Chummy, wasn't it? There's some tales I could tell you, though, that have never passed these lips before, and would make your hair curl.'

'Really, Tinker? Like what?' asked Beauchamp, flashing his hip flask for the fourth time and obligingly pouring a little soupcon – quite a large soupcon, actually – into Tinker's tankard, then waving it over his own, so that he served himself nothing more substantial than fumes.

'Very hospitable of you, Beechy. Wait up there!' the other requested, and toddled, slightly drunkenly, over to the door, to make sure that no one was eavesdropping. 'Can't be too careful, these days,' he added, and tapped the side of his nose with his right forefinger in a knowing gesture.

'There's a story about this fambly would fair knock you out, old son, an' I'm gonna share it with you today, cos you're my bes' mate, and I'm thinkin' of retiring' soon, so it don't matter a flyin' fig ter me wot anyone finks.' Tinker's speech was becoming a little slurred, not only because of the strength of the beer, but because of the constant addition of large measures of brandy to his drinking vessel.

'It 'appened when I was but a bit of a boy, 'ere, long, long ago.' A tear of alcohol-inspired emotion quivered at the corner of one eye, as he said this. 'It was when the major was only a captain, and 'e was posted abroad, but the missus wouldn't go wiv 'im. Don' know if you rem-em-em-ember tha''

'Of course I do, but you weren't quite a boy were you, because I'd just started as boot boy at Belchester Towers, and you're a good bit older than me,' replied Beauchamp, unable to completely stop himself from aiming for some accuracy.

'Wha'ever! Nearly two years, 'e was gorn, and 'er all alone 'ere. I got called out to do for 'im after only a coupla months – 'e 'ad a sort of local bungalow-y building 'e lived in by then – and you couldn't even make up what I saw when I was out there, with 'im, in forrin parts.'

'Only went and got 'isself married again, di'n't 'e. To a

native girl wot wasn't more 'n seventeen years old. Would you believe it, ol' son, ol' Beechy, ol' friend?'

'He didn't, Tinker! So what happened to her, this little foreign stunner?'

'She only went an' 'ad 'is baby, di'n't she.'

'Good grief!' exclaimed Beauchamp, trying not to let his voice boom out in his astonishment.

Tinker merely nodded sagely and drunkenly. 'Big-igamy, tha's wha' i' was. Big-ig-igamy!'

'So what did he do? Just leave her there when he got posted back to Blighty?' Beauchamp really was all ears. He'd never expected anything of this magnitude to come of his visit to see his old friend. What a motive for murder!

'Nuffink! Di'n't 'ave to. Arter she 'ad the nipper, 'er fambly sent 'er orf into the mountains, too ashamed to look their friends in the face again, what wiv 'er avin' a forrin baby an' all tha'. An' 'e just came swannin' back 'ere like nothin's 'appened. I reckon 'e was a right Pinkerton, don't you, Beechy?'

Beauchamp, who knew his *Madama Butterfly* but was surprised that Tinker did, nodded his head sagely in agreement, thinking that that little bombshell could be alive and well, and liable to burst on to the scene at any time, with no warning whatsoever. 'And has he never looked for them?' he asked, listening as intently as an Archers fan for the next instalment of the story.

'Nah! Said it was just a forrin bint, and that the marriage was a sham anyway, not bein' in English, like.'

'Well, bless my soul!' ejaculated Beauchamp, shocked to his very roots. This would make Lady Amanda's hair stand on end, when he told her later. 'I won't divulge this to another living soul,' he promised earnestly, his fingers crossed behind his back. And if Popeye had got wind of this, he wouldn't have to watch his tongue for much longer. That book really could be dynamite!

Hugo was also to be offered the roots of a family scandal by the wily old gamekeeper on the Fotherington-Flint land, but had a harder time finding his quarry. He knew where the gamekeeper's hut in the woods was, but, after squelching through the mud created by the thaw, earning himself boots that felt like they belonged in the Somme, so heavy were their soles, he found no one at home.

He stood rather disconsolately, as the trees dripped on him, calling out in his loudest voice, 'Rodgers! Rodgers!' that being the gamekeeper's name, but answer was there none. After a few efforts in this manner, with no answer whatsoever, he decided he'd better make for the house, but when he tried to walk, he found he couldn't get his shoes out of the ground. The thick covering of mud on the soles had melded into the mud below them, and stuck him faster than he had the strength to fight.

At this point, he changed tactics slightly, and began to shout, 'Help! Help!' Within less than a minute, a man had materialised like magic from a clump of trees and was walking towards him calling out, 'Hang on in there. I'm just coming.'

'Are you Rodgers?' asked Hugo, of this newly arrived stranger.

'I am, that,' replied the man, taking a good look at Hugo's predicament. 'You stay there a moment, and I'll just go and get something to release you. Very clayey, is this ground,' and disappeared off into the trees again.

By the time that Hugo had begun to wonder if the man had been a mirage born of panic, he returned with a spade in an old wheelbarrow. 'Soon have you out of there, old man. I'll take you back to the house, and we'll get your shoes cleaned up. Who have you come to see?'

'You actually,' answered Hugo, eyeing up the wheelbarrow suspiciously. He had a nasty idea that he knew what it was for.

'Deftly sliding the spade under Hugo's feet, one at a time, and trying to keep it as close to the actual sole as possible, Rodgers manage to break the suction and, having given Hugo a freedom of sorts, put the wheelbarrow behind him and gave him a deft little shove in the chest, so that he collapsed neatly into its interior.

'Quickest way, old man,' he consoled the humiliated Hugo, who merely sat in his new place of imprisonment, sighing and tutting. This was the second time he'd taken an undignified ride in a wheelbarrow this December, not to mention a barely remembered trip in the bucket of a mechanical digger, and it had to stop. He was feeling distinctly like a potato!

Lady Amanda, meanwhile, had tried to contact old Lady Mumbles, who had once been a big noise in the county before her husband lost everything gambling. She had had to sell up eventually, but made a game attempt to keep her property going by selling off the contents, bit by bit, and now lived with her niece just outside Belchester.

She was very chagrined indeed to find out, when she telephoned, that Lady Mumbles had, in fact, succumbed to an attack of influenza at the end of November, and had not survived the experience. She did find out from the niece, however, that her aunt had sold a lot of her possessions to F A Antiques in Belchester itself.

Thanking the niece and passing on her condolences, Lady Amanda ended the call and sat tapping a pen on the top of her desk, as she let her memory go for a stroll down its own personal lane. The name she wanted was in there somewhere; she just had to wait for it to surface before she could do anything else.

After a quarter of an hour of tapping and waiting, she suddenly shouted, 'Aha!' and dialled the number for Directory Enquiries. Within less than five minutes she was in contact with an auction house about a hundred and twenty-five miles from Belchester and, within another ten minutes, was in possession of the information that confirmed her, up to then, unsubstantiated suspicions.

Her next move would be to casually drop in on Donkey, on the pretext of seeking some feedback about the house tour that now seemed like years ago, instead of only a few days.

Hugo found himself in the pleasant fug of a large kitchen in the throes of baking day, and had gladly swapped his clay-caked shoes for a cup of (non-alcoholic) tea and a plate of chocolate biscuits – to raise his spirits after his unfortunate mishap, Mrs Hipkiss, the elderly housekeeper had said, as she set them before him on the kitchen table.

Hugo decided to play this hand perfectly straight, and he laid his cards on the table without a qualm. 'I'll be perfectly honest with you, Rodgers, Mrs Hipkiss, I am here to see if you have any knowledge whatsoever of a family scandal that would be ruinous, should it ever be made public.

'I don't do this alone. Lady Amanda and I are checking out several families of good name and status, because that wretched Capt Leslie Barrington-Blyss has written a book that he claimed would blow the lids off many of the families of this type.

'As you know, he was murdered on Boxing Day in Lady Amanda's library, and we have taken it upon ourselves, now that he's dead, to try to uncover what he might have found out. We are absolutely certain that his widow will halt publication. What we would like to do, however, as the only known copy of it, other than the one with his erstwhile publisher, is in the hands of the police, is to get there first, as it were, as any information you may be able to impart may be instrumental in uncovering the identity of his murderer.

'We don't want to leave Inspector Moody, whom we

165

consider to be incompetent, to muddle the case up, then let out details of what is contained in the book, to try to uncover the murderer. It would be advantageous to everyone if we could solve the case first, and save many families untold embarrassment. At the very least, it will give those involved sufficient time to take out an injunction against the contents of this execrable tome being made public.'

Hugo finished his speech just before the point where he talked himself into a state in which he didn't understand, any more, what he was talking about, and was surprised when his audience of two began to clap their hand in appreciation.

'Noble words! Fine fellow! And Lady Amanda, too!' Rodgers congratulated Hugo's sentiments.

'May God bless you, Mr Hugo!' added Mrs Hipkiss, before looking at Rodgers to see if he had anything to offer.

'Sorry,' the gamekeeper apologised. 'I'm afraid I can't think of anything that would count as a big scandal likely to do damage to the Fotherington-Flint name. I wish I could help you, but I can't.'

Hugo sighed, and transferred his gaze to Mrs Hipkiss, who was looking doubtful. 'Well,' she mused, 'there's nothing in my time, and I'm as old as Mrs Methuselah; but my mother worked here before I did, and I think, if you give me a minute or two to get my head together about it, I might – I just might – nothing definite – have something for you.'

Hugo, ever a patient soul, dunked his biscuits happily, and accepted a refill of his teacup, as Mrs Hipkiss wracked her brains to recall a tale told to her decades ago, and which she hadn't thought much about since. Eventually, she gave a yell of, 'Got it!' and pulled up a chair opposite the unexpected visitor to her kitchen.

'Oh, it was donkey's years ago, ducky,' she began, 'and

it wasn't to do with the present Sir Montacute, but his parents, young lovers that they were, then. Still teenagers, and not married, although betrothed and properly engaged, his mother-to-be suddenly disappeared from sight. She never left her parents' house for months on end, and a story was circulated that she was gravely ill.

'Meanwhile, the wedding was planned, but there were those that believed she'd never be well enough to attend the ceremony.' Hugo was already enthralled, and sat with his chin in one hand, his mouth slightly open, with what Lady A referred to as his 'catching flies' face.

'My mother was good friends with her mother's maid at the time – they used to spend all their half-days together – and her friend told her of the awful weeping and screaming that had gone on about a week before that girl was seen in public once more. Her friend had been convinced that she was in her death throes.

'My mother, she was altogether more sceptical, and she remembered how that girl's mother had called at this house the same night that her friend reported the weeping and screaming, and my mother distinctly heard her mother say just a few words. 'It's a girl. It's already gone for private adoption.

'Well, I can tell you what my mother deduced. That the young couple had put the cart before the horse, and now the mess was being sorted out for them by their parents. The wedding went ahead about three months later, and it was less than a year before they produced our own Sir Montacute, but none of this has got anything to do with him. He wasn't even born at the time.'

'Eh?' grunted Hugo. 'Is that the end of the story? Couldn't you tell me another one, please? I was really enjoying myself there.'

Lady Amanda was shown through immediately to the drawing room of The Old Convent, where she found

Angelica Featherstonehaugh-Armitage already in the arms of a cocktail, and thoroughly enjoying the experience.

'Manda! How lovely to see you again!' she brayed, putting down her glass and coming forward to embrace her unexpected guest fondly. 'Take a seat and I'll get you a dry martini. I know how you love your cocktails.'

'Please don't bother on my account,' countered Lady Amanda. 'Got to watch the old digestion after all that rich food over the festive season, but don't let me stop you.'

Taking this as an invitation, Angelica swayed over to the cocktail cabinet and fixed herself another drink, calling over her shoulder, 'And to what do I owe the honour of this visit?'

'Just thought I'd drop in and see what you thought of the old tour of the Towers, you know. Stinky not about?'

'Absolutely not! He went up to his club for a couple of days after that dreadful incident in your library, but I'm expecting him back tonight.'

A voice in Lady Amanda's head yelled, 'Yippee!' although she wasn't quite sure why this part of her mind was so pleased. She'd ask it later. Instead, adopting a very casual air, she enquired after the antiques business that the lieutenant colonel used to run.

'I never did ask you why Stinky relinquished the old antiques game in North Street. Wanted to retire, did he, and just gave it up?' she purred casually.

'Not a bit of it,' replied Angelica, absorbing her dry martini in the manner of a parched sponge. 'It was more like *it* gave *him* up. Dammit! Empty glass again! I was sure I'd just mixed myself one.'

As her host returned to the cocktail shaker (for, like James Bond, she preferred hers shaken, not stirred) Lady Amanda cast her bread upon the waters and asked temptingly, 'Whatever do you mean? I can't see how that can have happened,' then added, 'It's so rare that you and I get the chance to have a good old girlie chinwag, Donkey old sport.'

'You're right, there,' replied Donkey, the bread and hook firmly in her mouth. 'I'll tell you all about it, and you can see how it went from fabulously profitable to absolute zilch in just a few short years.'

With an internal grin of triumph, Lady Amanda relaxed back in her armchair and prepared to make mental notes.

'When he first started in the business – that was when he took over from his father, and he himself had just come out of the army – things were selling like hot cakes. Whatever he bought was snapped up in the craze for Victoriana. I remember, in particular, that even a broken gout stool and a dilapidated fire-screen fetched unheard-of sums.

'Then the bottom fell out of Victoriana, so he turned to Georgian and Regency items, specialising in furniture and pictures – he isn't really a bibelot man, as I'm sure you can appreciate. Then we hit the present, seemingly endless, slump, and the bottom fell out of brown furniture.' At this point, she went off into screeches of hysterical laughter at her own humour, calming down again only to return to mix herself another martini, muttering, 'Bottom fell out – heehee. Clunk, ouch! Heeheehee!'

'So how did you manage?' asked Lady Amanda, determined to get her on to more solid ground, and not let her disappear with a bad case of barman's elbow.

'Couldn't believe it myself, but, for a while, it was horrible old pictures. Stinky had quite a lot of luck with them. Filthy old daubs, they looked to me, but he'd go off to a country auction or whatever, and come back with these horrible things, and the next thing we knew, one or two of them had sold for a fabulous sum at auction. Boy, did that man have an eye.'

'To the main chance,' muttered Lady Amanda inaudibly. This was what she'd come to hear, having spoken to the niece of the poor, dear, departed Lady

Mumbles, and the auction house. That man had an eye, all right, but it wasn't for a picture, it was for a sucker, and one who trusted him because of who he was. He'd out-and-out swindled old Lady Mumbles in her hour of need, and, no doubt, she wasn't his only victim.

When Lady A looked across at Donkey, after this momentary pause for thought, she saw her eyes droop, and her martini glass along with it. Quietly removing the latter and placing it on a handy side-table, she tiptoed from the room and left the house. It was lucky she had caught Donkey in a 'relaxed' mood, as it had saved her the bother of being too wily in her quest to loosen the woman's tongue – so naive, and so trusting, that she was.

Back at 'the ranch', all three of its occupants had tales to tell and, checking that she wouldn't disturb any plans for dinner, Lady Amanda convened a meeting to share the intelligence they had gathered that day, and requested that Beauchamp might like to join them in a cocktail for this gathering.

Beauchamp arrived promptly with the drinks tray, but Hugo was tardy by a good two minutes. 'Sorry!' he called as he came through the door, having been taken short unexpectedly again, by a call of nature on his amble along from his bedroom, then went flying across the carpet, as he tripped, just inside the doorway.

Beauchamp rushed to his rescue, ascertaining that he was uninjured, just rather surprised and shaken. As he helped the man to his feet, Hugo said accusingly, 'I fell over your blasted handbag, Manda. What do you think you're doing just dropping it on the floor where anyone could fall over it?'

'I'm so sorry,' she replied, real chagrin in her voice. 'It's just that I've learnt some things that I'm finding it hard to come to terms with, and I suppose I just abandoned it without thinking. My apologies, old stick.'

'Well, be more careful in future. Thing like that could kill a man.'

'I know, Hugo, and I'm so pleased you haven't broken anything,' she replied.

'You should take a look at my dignity. It's shattered into a thousand pieces on the floor. What on earth do you keep in the thing, bricks? It weighs a ton.'

'Only what I deem absolutely essential,' she replied with dignity.

'And why would you carry around a couple of house bricks? Come on, what have you really got in it. Show me.' Hugo had never examined the contents of a lady's handbag before, and was now genuinely interested.

'Pass it here,' she asked, then began to intone, as she removed items from it, 'Lipstick, mirror, face powder, small bottle of perfume, address book, mobile phone, house keys, screwdriver, apple corer, wire cutters, scissors, sewing kit, fifteen metre metal tape-measure, crochet hook, pen, pencil, cross-hatch screwdriver, small hacksaw, paint brush, nail polish, manicure set …'

'Manda!' Hugo exclaimed, although there were still items left in the bag. 'Are you sure you haven't got a cement mixer in there too? It's as well-equipped as a tool box. Why on earth do you carry all that stuff around with you?'

'Because it's all very useful stuff, and I never know when I might need a hacksaw or a screwdriver. The apple-corer I use all the time. So useful for a healthy snack if one is on the move.'

'Well, I have to hand it to you; you would have made a marvellous boy scout. Be prepared? You're more than that, but I don't think I could be bothered lugging such a heavy receptacle around with me wherever I go.'

'That's the difference between men and women, Hugo. When a woman needs something unexpectedly, she can usually find it in her handbag. When a man wants something unexpectedly, he usually asks his lady companion if she's got such a thing in her bag.'

'Touché! I surrender!' Hugo retired from the battlefield with a good grace, nursing his wounds without rancour.

'Any luck, chaps?' she asked, when they were all settled round the fire with a drink apiece. Receiving a pair of answers in the affirmative, she told them to fire away, and listened with round eyes to what they had gleaned from their visits.

At the end of it, she availed herself of a, 'Well, I'll be blowed,' then set out to summarize what they had learned so far. 'Let's start with the Heyhoe-Caramacs. We'd all heard about his father being a war hero and his work with the Resistance in France, but from what has been turned up, it would seem that there is a strong possibility that he collaborated with the Germans, and was the cause of several civilian deaths. Unbelievable!' she added, 'but probably absolutely true. Unsubstantiated rumours are often disproved as merely malicious, while the guilty truth is guarded like Fort Knox.

'Next, we'll look at what we've discovered about the ffolliat DeWinters – good work there, Beauchamp, with old Fustion. No one ever suspected there was anything suspect about ffolliat DeWinter senior's death, because he had been so ill, was a reckless old fool with his health, and would heed advice from no one.

'Now, it would seem, that he was given a helping hand into the afterlife by his loving son and daughter-in-law. Of course, there's nothing to disprove that he wouldn't have popped off that very day, but the old fellow, knowing how stubborn he was, might have hung about for years, and those two obviously had pressing financial problems that couldn't wait.

'Mapperley-Minto's behaviour while abroad seems to be completely beyond the pale, and if that book were published, it was more than likely that the tale would be examined in minute detail, and his 'not-wife' and illegitimate child traced. Utter disgrace!

'Still, at least it kept him out of Maddy's bed for more than a twelve-month. I did hear that he was a real old lecher when he'd had a few drinks to relax him, and she really couldn't be doing with that sort of thing.'

'Manda!' exclaimed Hugo, at this, in his opinion, totally unnecessary foray into bedroom habits.

'It's true! She told me once! First time I've ever mentioned it, though,' pleaded Lady Amanda, in her own defence. With a regal shake of her head, to clarify her thoughts after this interruption, she went on, 'Next, we come to the Fotherington-Flints, and that's where I've been doing some investigation, with a little help from our friendly neighbourhood policeman, PC Glenister, who was able to obtain access that was denied to me, to certain records.'

'But I did that one!' cried Hugo, in distress. 'It was me – I – who found out that Sir Montacute's parents had an illegitimate baby and gave it away to private adoption.' He felt righteously indignant that Manda should steal his thunder so.

'I know, Hugo, but it was I who found out that fate conspired for them to meet years later and marry.'

'No!'

'Impossible!'

'I know how you both feel. The machinations of a malevolent fate make my toes curl, but that's the truth of the matter. I don't think they found out until long after their marriage, but old sins have long shadows, and there's always someone, somewhere, who knows the truth. I have a feeling that they've been living in a brother/sister relationship for a very long time, dreading the truth coming out.

'No wonder Daisy tries to act younger than her years, being, in fact, older than him, and that Cutie has grown so grumpy in his later years, learning the truth about his wife's parentage, having believed she was a product of the parents who had adopted her.

'That only leaves us with the Featherstonehaugh-Armitages, and I confirmed the goods on old Stinky today. He was swindling trusting customers who came to him to sell some of their heirlooms when their circumstances became straitened. They trusted him because of where he stood in society, and he let them down completely, telling them that their pictures were copies, or their precious pieces of furniture were reproductions, and that their jewellery was paste.

'When confronted with their disbelief, he told the old story; that their forebears had only done what they were attempting to do now, but actually replacing the originals with copies, so that they wouldn't lose any face to the world at large. Isn't that beastly, to cheat your own kind?' she asked, then concluded with, 'Well, that's the lot of them, and I bet Mouldy Moody's having a field day, running his grubby little eyes over that lot!'

'It's not quite all, Manda,' said Hugo, softly.

'What do you mean, not all. Isn't that enough to be going on with?' What else could there possibly be?'

'You!' he said, looking her sorrowfully in the face. 'What about all the goings on in this family over the years? If Popeye got wind of that, he'd have thought he'd won the football pools.'

'I think you'll find it's the Lottery, these days, Mr Hugo,' interjected Beauchamp, but with his face creased with anxiety.

'Don't forget,' Hugo went on, 'Your mother's still alive and living in Monte Carlo, and she's living proof of all that went on in this family.'

'Oh, my God!' whispered Lady Amanda, more to herself than to her two companions.

'So who did it, Manda? Which one of them killed

174

Popeye?'

'I haven't the faintest idea,' she replied. 'All I know is that it wasn't me.'

The sombre mood was broken at that juncture by a heavy knocking at the front door, and the sound of someone pulling frantically at the bell-pull, and Beauchamp left the room in thoughtful mood to answer the summons.

Inspector Moody stood in front of the fire unashamedly warming his buttocks as he addressed them, PC Glenister standing just inside the door, in the remote case that one of them would make a run for it. Moody wasn't taking any chances with his run-in with a higher social circle: he didn't trust them further than he could throw his car.

'I don't care if you find it distasteful. I insist that it be done. If anyone can blag their way through a believable tale, it's you,' he said, fixing Lady Amanda with a gimlet eye. 'I want the whole lot reassembled in the library tomorrow, so that I can say my piece.' And what a piece it was too. He was almost bursting with pride at his deductions, as well as his literary knowledge. He'd always wanted to gather the suspects in a case in a library, and give it to them with both barrels.

'If you won't comply with my request, I shall arrest the lot of you, and do it down the station,' he threatened, intoning the last three words in a sepulchral voice, to emphasize the gravity of the situation.

After the departure of the two representatives of the law, Lady Amanda went to the telephone and consulted her address book. If it had to be done, it had to be done, and there wasn't a thing she could do to prevent it.

Chapter Fifteen
Hugo Pulls it Off

The following afternoon, with the exception of Capt. Leslie Barrington-Blyss, the same guests who had assembled so hopefully on Boxing Day gathered again at Belchester Towers, but this time they were a subdued crowd, with hardly a word to say to each other. There was the smell of fear in the air, as they moved, for the second time that Christmastide, through to the library. Enid Tweedie, too, was in attendance, and in charge of refreshments, but these were simple today, as Beauchamp had thought that nobody would feel much like eating and drinking.

When they had all settled in seats, an utter silence filled the room as Lady Amanda announced that Inspector Moody would be joining them, as she had explained on the telephone the night before. There had been several cases of insomnia in and around Belchester the night before, at the prospect of what this little gathering would reveal.

PC Glenister, as usual, was in the background, as Moody began pompously, perhaps imagining himself to be Hercule Poirot, 'I have asked you to return to the scene of the recent murder of one of your number, because I have several things to say which will, I am sure, lead to the unmasking of whoever committed this terrible crime.'

'I have read Captain Barrington-Blyss's book in its entirety, and, in that manuscript, I have found several motives for murder, should certain things be made public. 'You!' he suddenly shouted, pointing at Lt Col. Featherstonehaugh-Armitage. 'You borrowed money from your father's business before he died, and I know you didn't have permission. How would that look to the public eye, stealing from a sick old man? Eh? Eh?'

Stinky and Donkey merely looked at each other and smiled, shrugging their shoulders as they did so. 'If you say so,' retorted Stinky, looking more cheerful than he had since he arrived, and causing Moody to crease his brow in puzzlement. This wasn't how it was supposed to happen. They were supposed to look scared and guilty.

He ploughed on, nevertheless, turning his attention, next, to Sir Montacute Fotherington-Flint. 'You, sir, used to poach on your father's land, and sell the valuable game birds to a restaurant thirty miles away, under a false name. Not only is poaching illegal, but what you did was out and out theft, then you fenced the proceeds to a restaurant.'

Cutie managed a wry smile, and invited the inspector to 'pick the bones out of that one'. This laid-back attitude to criminal accusations was anathema to Moody. They should be quaking in their boots at the thought of prosecution, not to mention what else he had up his sleeve, not treating his statements as if they were an everyday occurrence, and of no consequence whatsoever. His law-abiding soul was scandalised.

'And you!' he suddenly roared, this time indicating Major Mapperley-Minto. You cheated at cards. I have it all in black and white that you were a card cheat, and you can't deny it.'

'I don't propose to do so,' replied Monty coolly, his face a mask of relief. 'But I had my reasons.'

'There's no excuse for what you did!' roared Moody, now beginning to feel his ship, which had just come in for him, beginning to sink beneath his feet. His voice rising a little as he lost a bit of nerve, he next singled out Sir Jolyon ffolliat DeWinter. 'You were caught out having forged your father's signature on a cheque. A more despic …'

At this point Hugo, feeling vastly relieved, began to tune out the hysterical accusations of the inspector. Old Popeye may have thought he had social dynamite between the covers of his book, but all he'd really had were a few damp squibs. He'd never really got down to the real dirt, to reveal the skeletons in the family closets, and Moody was ranting and railing to no avail. He'd get no change out of that lot.

As he mused to himself, he found his eyes lighting on a black patent leather handbag, sitting at the feet of Fifi and, given his uncommonly close encounter with one of those contraptions, and Manda's revealing tour of the contents of hers, he wondered what weird and wonderful things she carried around with her. It wasn't as big as Manda's, but he had realised, the day before, that handbags were invariably bigger on the inside than they were on the outside, a fact that had escaped his notice all these years.

His eyes moved on to Maddie M-M's, and found it to be roughly the same size as that of Fifi's. This one was red suede, with little flowers embroidered on it, and he wondered that he had never looked at these everyday workhorses before, in all their various guises.

Becoming thoroughly interested, now, he carried on moving his eyes from woman to woman, taking notice of their taste in such receptacles, and idly musing what one would find, should one venture to open them.

Moody had not noticed that Hugo had fallen into a brown study, and was carrying on with his tirade. 'And as for you,' he shouted, pointing at Col. Heyhoe-Caramac. 'What sort of man beats his dog? I shall be informing the RSPCA about what I've learnt of your behaviour towards animals.'

At this point, now wild-eyed, as he slowly became aware that nobody was listening to him any more, and had begun to talk amongst themselves, he raised his voice as loud as he could and yelled, 'I know who killed the captain!'

This certainly drew attention back to him as, his face red, his hair rumpled where he had run his hands through it at the thought that they could have ignored him at such an important part of this denouement, he prepared to *reveal all*. His mouth wide open, he declared in a bellow, 'It was all of you! Every single one of you, or at least in pairs. Did you think I didn't notice what a case of overkill it was? He was poisoned! He was stabbed! He was garrotted! He was hit over the head! And his throat was cut!

'Do you honestly think that I never read *Murder on the Orient Express*? Did you think you could fool me that easily? You all had adequate motive to do away with him, and I think you got together and planned the whole thing. Do you know how long you can get in prison for conspiracy? And I haven't finished yet, not by a long chalk!' He now looked and sounded like a raving lunatic.

Hugo, meanwhile, had continued his visual examination of the various handbags in laps and on the floor of the library, and was just beginning to appreciate how much better than pockets they were. One could carry so much in them without disturbing the line of the cut of one's clothes. One could simply put them down, without having to go around with a load of clunky things in one's pockets.

He had just decided what a jolly good idea they were, and was quite chagrined that men could not use them, when his eyes fell on Porky's bag, and a small light went on at the back of his mind, accompanied by the almost inaudible tinkle of a very small bell.

The bag was so small that he had hardly noticed it, propped up against an ankle: what he thought was referred to as a clutch bag, which could contain little more than keys and a lipstick. On Boxing Day, he had been impressed by the size of the tapestry bag she toted around with her, thinking it as big as Manda's, and here she was today, with something in which it would be impossible to keep even something as bulky as a hair brush.

All around him, Inspector Moody was being conspicuously ignored as the guests lost themselves in happy chatter. When Enid had gone round earlier with sausage rolls and mince pies, she had received a universal refusal. As she circulated, once more, in this vastly relieved atmosphere, with her little snacks, the uptake was a hundred per cent, as was Beauchamp's offer of glasses of sherry. Both snacks and drinks were being relished as the babble of conversation rose in volume, to the 'rhubarb, rhubarb' chorus present in any parliamentary broadcast, and Moody was on his feet now, about to explode with wrath at this disrespectful attitude to one of his rank.

The light at the back of Hugo's brain suddenly glowed like phosphorus, and the bell rang with the sonorous tones of its campanological brother, Big Ben. It was all to do with handbags! The book was involved in there somewhere, but the clue to the murderer was a handbag, and he believed he had just had a revelation.

As Moody called for silence, Hugo sprang, as quickly as he could manage, from a sitting position, and yelled, 'It's her!'

All eyes were swivelled to look in the direction in which he was pointing, to reveal Porky, her face as white as a sheet, and opening and closing her mouth like a landed fish.

'What the hell do you think you're saying, you doddering old fart?' spat Moody, as Lady Amanda called out, 'Explain yourself, Hugo! What was Porky? What are you saying? Tell me this instant.'

'Not until I've asked a couple of questions first,' replied Hugo rebelliously. He would not have his thunder stolen; no one was going to rain on his parade today. The library, now, was absolutely silent as he spoke. 'Porky, I would like to know the name of the publishing house with which Popeye was dealing,' he demanded in a much more forceful voice than was usual for him.

'That's none of your damned business, Chummy!' she retorted, looking daggers at him.

'And how are your finances at the moment? I would have thought that Popeye would have had a rather plump advance from a publisher who thought he was exploding a social bomb.'

'That's none of your damned business either, you nosy old fool.'

'What are you talking about, Hugo?' asked Lady Amanda, not having caught the direction of his thoughts yet.

'We've heard, courtesy of the well-read inspector here today, about the sensitive information that was in Popeye's book, and from the attitude in this room now, I think that we can take it that it's not worth a penny.'

'Hear, hear!' shouted Major Mapperley-Minto. 'I admit that I did cheat at cards, but only when I was playing with her husband. I spotted him first off as a card-sharp, and I was determined to play him at his own game. Apart from the few games we played together, and he soon stopped asking me if I fancied a hand, I have never cheated at cards in my life.'

Everyone was clamouring to have their say now, and it was Sir Jolyon ffolliat DeWinter who wrested the floor from the others, next. 'As for that signature on my father's cheque, it was one he had meant to sign before he went away on business for a couple of days, but if I hadn't settled the debt, I would have been in real trouble. I was only a young stripling, and when the bank questioned the signature, my father backed me to the hilt, and said he had been feeling rather shaky that day, and the signature was, in fact, his.'

'And with reference to my poaching, my father knew what I was up to, but never said anything until years later, when he explained he had kept quiet because he didn't want me to end up a rotten shot like old Bonkers.'

At this moment, Colonel Henry Heyhoe-Caramac shot him an evil glance, and rose to his feet for his moment of justification. 'I may have been a bit rough when I trained the dog to which you were referring, but only with a rolled up newspaper, and that training wasn't a waste of time. When I fell off the barn roof, it was dear old Stumpy who went back to the house and barked his head off until someone would follow him. I'd gashed my leg badly on the way down, and if it hadn't been for that dog, I'd have bled to death. So there!'

Lt Col. Featherstonehaugh-Armitage now stood, taking his turn in the limelight. If everyone else was going to explain away their apparent misdemeanours, he didn't see why he shouldn't have his turn too.

'My father had no idea that I'd 'borrowed' money from the family business, for the simple reason that he had what we refer to now as Alzheimer's, but in those days, was referred to as 'senile dementia'. My mother wanted it kept as quiet as possible, because she felt it would bring shame on the family – you know how people used to think in those days.

'Anyway, as co-signatory on the account, she very kindly loaned me the money until I could pay it back, which was something my father never could have done, because he didn't even know who I was, by that time. Does that satisfy you, Inspector bloody Moody?'

In the meantime, Lady Amanda had made her way across to the unpopular policeman, and in the guise of offering him some words of comfort at this sudden implosion of his multiple-murderer theory, whispered in his ear, 'If you say one word about the Golightly family, I shall have you in court so quickly on a defamation of character and slander charge that your feet won't touch the ground, sonny!'

She then went to the middle of the room and requested that Hugo go on with his accusation.

Hugo, in fine form now, took the floor once more and declared, as if in court, 'It is my belief that Porky brought that huge handbag with her on Boxing Day because of financial irregularities on the part of her husband, and that, in it, she had secreted all the weapons that were used on her husband in his murder.

'Her intention was to confuse and confound, for she knew how unpopular he was. She relied on this unpopularity, so that some dolt,' at this point, he looked at Moody, 'would come to the conclusion that all the guests were in collusion, and had conspired to kill him.

'I expect that you will find something in her house – maybe a bronze, or something of that sort – with which she brained him. He was garrotted, and the cord or wire, or whatever was used, must have been cut from somewhere. I suggest her garden shed be examined in minute detail. His throat was also cut. I put it to you,' he was in fine courtroom drama form now, 'that he was stabbed with the knife that also cut his throat, and that that knife was none other than the one he used at his own desk for opening mail. I'm sure I've seen it somewhere before, and I'm fairly certain it was in his house.'

At this, there was a general murmur of agreement, which really gratified Hugo, as he hadn't been in Popeye's house for a very long time, and was actually winging it now. 'As for the poison, may I suggest a thorough rummage through the greenhouse might throw up an old week-killing product that contains something now banned?'

Porky raised her considerable bulk from the chair and spat across the room, 'You foul old fiend. How did you know all that?'

'Because you've just confirmed it for me, thank you very much,' replied Hugo, not forgetting his manners, even in the face of melodrama.

PC Glenister moved unobtrusively from his position in the background and slickly applied handcuffs to Porky's wrists, before looking towards his superior for instructions as to how he should proceed.

Moody had grabbed a sherry with each hand from Beauchamp's beckoning tray, and was too busy pouring them down his throat to even acknowledge that he had noticed what Glenister had done.

It was, or course, Lady Amanda who took charge of the situation, nodding to Beauchamp to stay where he was, while the inspector quenched his thirst at his leisure, although it seemed a pity to see such a fine old sherry being downed as if it were cordial.

'Come on, Porky, spill the beans. Why did you really do it? Was it all down to money? I thought you were loaded. In fact, I thought that was why Popeye married you in the first place,' she asked baldly.

'I was loaded. Back then. But I had no idea how Popeye had been getting through the money, and when I went Christmas shopping just a while ago, I had my bank card refused in two shops before I thought to call into the bank to see what the problem was. The problem was that there was next to nothing left in our account, because Popeye had spent it all. And he'd always been so mean and frugal with me.

'I went off home in a rage, and on the way I thought that all he could talk about for months had been this bloody book of his, so I thought I'd have a little rifle through his drawers when he next went out, so that I could work out if he'd just borrowed a chunk of it temporarily, while waiting for his advance cheque to arrive.

'Boy, was I a sucker! There was no advance cheque. All I found in his desk were rejection letters from over a score of publishers. The only contract I could lay my hands on was from a vanity publishing house, which he was actually paying to print the bloody thing, and he'd ordered thousands and thousands of copies, as if he wanted to stock every book shop in the country. That's where the last of the money went!

'I was in such a rage that I felt almost calm. I opened up the computer and began to read what he had written – something of which he probably didn't think I was capable – and it was absolutely terrible. It wasn't just that he didn't have enough dynamite to blow his own nose, it was the grammar and the spelling too. And talk about purple prose. If he paid for that to be published – and with my money, I might add – he'd be a laughing stock, and a broke one at that.

'I rang the publishing house after checking the cheque book, and told them I'd put a stop on the cheque, and they weren't to go ahead with anything until I said so, and if they didn't do what I asked, I'd go to the papers about them publishing a book that was likely to attract some notoriety in the courts, because all those mentioned in it would sue the pants off both the author and his publisher. I was absolutely incandescent with fury.

'And, I wasn't quite prepared to face poverty without even the company of my old friends, and he had some hefty insurance policies on his life, so I just thought, why not? Why not remove the only fly in the ointment of my life, and at least preserve what little money I had left and collect on the insurance?'

There was a general chorus of, 'Porky!'

'Don't you dare look down your noses at me! What was I supposed to do? Take it all in good part and put my name on the list for social housing? I'd certainly no hopes of maintenance if I divorced him, so the only way out I could see was to do away with him completely. Why are you all looking so shocked? None of you liked him!'

Constable Glenister helped Porky to her feet, moved over to where Inspector Moody was sitting and pulled him by the shoulder of his mackintosh until he stood up. He turned briefly towards the assembled company and wished them a cheery 'good day' before making his exit, on his return journey back to the police station. Once outside, he unlocked the car, ushered his prisoner into the back seat, then opened the passenger door for the inspector. 'I think I'd better drive, don't you, sir?' he asked, removing his helmet before assisting the broken man into the car.

Chapter Sixteen
OMG – Again!

After seeing the thunderstruck guests off the premises, Lady Amanda, Hugo and Enid gathered in the drawing room, waiting for Beauchamp to join them with a tray of cocktails, not only because it was 'cocktail o'clock', but because they had had a very trying afternoon, and needed a little kick to revive them.

'I say, Manda, who would have thought it of poor old Porky?' declared Hugo, a smile of victory hovering around his lips.

'Well, *you* obviously, you cunning old bloodhound, you. How on earth did you work it out?' retorted Lady Amanda, looking a shade jealous of Hugo's revelations in the library.

'I wouldn't have given it a thought, if I hadn't tripped over your handbag, old thing. Sort of put the things in my mind, so to speak, and when that dreary little inspector was droning on about the pathetic contents of Popeye's book, I just let my eyes and mind wander, examining the women's bags and comparing them.

'Yours had contained what appeared to be the entire contents of a garden shed and make-up counter combined, and I wondered how much stuff other women carried round with them. I thought I was getting quite a feel for colour and style, when my eyes lit on Porky's bag. I don't know if you noticed it, but it was one of those tiny things that you can tuck under one arm. Is it a clutch bag?' he asked.

'Where on earth did you learn so much about ladies'

189

handbags, Hugo?' Enid asked, making him blush.

'Just the sort of thing that one picks up, you know? Anyway, there was something at the back of my head that said that bag was somehow wrong, and I didn't have the faintest idea why I should think such a thing, when I had a vision of this vast tapestry bag, and realised that when she was here on Boxing Day, she had had an absolutely enormous specimen with her. Then I suddenly lighted on why she needed such a big one.'

'To carry all the necessary weapons to make it look like a crowd of people had murdered her husband,' supplied Lady Amanda. 'And I actually saw her put her gloves into it when she arrived, so now we know why there were no fingerprints on anything. It did fleetingly cross my mind, with them being so obviously at loggerheads with each other, that she might have chosen that one just to annoy him, but then I thought no more of it, with so much going on. Clever old Hugo!

'I must say, I've heard of crowds of people being massacred by a lunatic individual, and an individual being massacred by a crowd, but a massacre being committed by one person on only one other is really bizarre. But how ingenious of her to think of it in the first place!'

'Manda!' Hugo admonished her. 'The poor woman's going to prison for murder. Have you no sympathy?'

'Not really. She should have kept a closer eye on her finances if they had joint accounts. She was the one who had the money when they married, and she should have been more aware of what was going on; and made regular checks. Anyway, as Popeye's book hasn't already flooded the market, she can claim that his death nullifies the contract, and will have no problem with the cancelled cheque, although I suppose that's the least of her worries at the moment. Now, where's that man? BEAUCHaargh! There you are! You nearly scared the life out of me, Beauchamp.'

'That's Beecham, my lady!' the manservant retorted softly.

'No it's not, and I'm not deaf, you know. Not yet, anyway. I heard exactly what you said. So, what have you got for us tonight, then? Something appropriate, I hope,' she asked, rubbing her hands together in anticipation.

'I have a White Christmas for you again, my lady and a Wobbly Knee for Mr Hugo, as he's still suffering. It might, perhaps, have been more appropriate to serve him with a Little White Lie, but I don't think the police suspected anything when he said he'd seen the knife on the captain's desk.'

Hugo turned red and smiled at the same time. 'First time for everything, what?' he retorted.

'And for Mrs Enid and myself, I have made a Best Year, and I think I can say that, with all the changes that have taken place this year, it has been the best for a very long time.'

'Well said, Beauchamp! Here's to the Fearless Four, and to more detecting. It's certainly put a spring in my step and some zest in my life! Cheers!'

As they drank, there came a loud knocking on the front door, and Lady Amanda looked at the clock with astonishment. She had issued no other invitations for the day, and she was sure that Inspector Moody was probably still breaking pencils and climbing the walls in his frustration, at this very moment. Who on earth could it be?

'I'll get it,' volunteered Enid. 'You stay here and enjoy your cocktail, Beau ... Beech ... ham,' she compromised on his name, not daring to choose one body of opinion over the other.

At the door she found an elderly moustachioed gentleman in a bowler hat and camel hair coat who thrust a business card at her, and apologised for arriving without an appointment, but that he had to see Lady Amanda with the utmost urgency.

Enid took the card, held it at arm's length to read it, and said, 'Do come in, Mr Bradshaigh.'

'That's Bradshaw!' the man retorted, slightly miffed at this pronunciation. 'Can't you read, woman?'

'I certainly can, Mr Bradshaigh, and 'Bradshaigh' it says on this card,' and then she lost her temper. 'I've had Cholmondley that's pronounced Chummley, Crichton that's pronounced Cryton, Featherstonehaugh that's pronounced Fanshaw, and now you say you're Bradshaigh, pronounced Bradshaw. What sort of schools did your forebears go to? I ask myself. Mine went to a place that taught them to read what was in front of them, and not miss out half the syllables, and then just make up the rest of them!' and she stamped her foot in exasperation before she recovered her manners.

'Follow me into the drawing room where I'm sure everybody will be able to read your name with complete accuracy,' she replied in high dudgeon, and stomped off, a rather surprised Mr Bradshaigh trailing in her wake, totally flummoxed by Enid's spirited outburst of confusion and anger.

At the door, she announced, 'There's a Mr Bradshaigh who says his name's pronounced Bradshaw, to see you. Here is his card,' and with that, she sat down again and threw the rest of her cocktail down her throat defiantly.

'Mr Bradshaigh,' Lady Amanda welcomed him, with perfect pronunciation. 'How nice to see you again, but it must be twenty years since we last met. What brings you here so unexpectedly? Mama's solicitor,' she added, so that the other three knew who he was.

'It's about your mother,' he began, but was stopped in his tracks as Lady Amanda interrupted him.

'But Mama's been dead these twenty years. What business can you have, concerning her affairs?'

'I know she's not dead, Lady Amanda. I was in on the

plot. How could she live abroad under another name without someone to manage her finances for her? I've been in the background all this time, quietly working away at her behest. But, to cut a long story short,' he said, noting that Lady Amanda's mouth was hanging open at the thought of someone else (other than Beauchamp) who had known about her mother faking her own death, when she herself knew nothing.

'Whatever's the man talking …' began Enid, but was immediately silenced by one of Lady A's glares, and her almost spat instruction.

'Enid, you will repeat nothing whatsoever that is taking place in this room now, to another living soul, and if you do, I know where you live, and I will hunt you down and kill you like a dog. Do I make myself crystal clear?'

'Absolutely, Lady Amanda. No word shall ever pass my lips. I swear on my mother's life that I shall be mute for the rest of my life.' Enid felt a shiver of genuine fear move through her body at Lady Amanda's vehemence.

Mr Bradshaigh, having remained silent while Lady Amanda set out her absolute demand for silence, continued without turning a hair, 'To cut a long story short, your mother is on her deathbed with pneumonia and a chest infection, and I had a call from the hospital on my mobile to tell me that she was fading fast. If you want to see her again, alive, you'll have to move quickly.'

The mood in the drawing room grew sombre, as Lady Amanda asked, 'Is that all you know?'

'I know that she's written a letter for you, in case you're too late, and that she asked that you be informed that you're not an only child. Either she, or her letter, will explain, when you get there.'

'WHAT?' Lady Amanda was on her feet. '*Not an only child*? I've *always* been an only child. Ever since I was *born*! Has the woman *finally* lost her marbles? Where's the *proof*? Inventing phantom children like that! Well, it simply won't *do*! I *demand* to know what's happening!'

THE END

Read on for cocktail recipes from this story!

AFTERWORD

Cocktail Recipes

White Christmas
1 measure crème de banana
1 measure white crème de cacao
1 measure scotch whisky
1 measure double cream
Shake and strain, sprinkle with grated chocolate

Wobbly Knee
1 measure Amaretto di Saronno
1 measure Kahlua
1/2 measure vodka
3/4 measure coconut cream
1 measure double cream
Blend briefly with a glassful of crushed ice, sprinkle with grated chocolate

Bumpo
2 measures golden rum
1 measure lime juice
1 tsp caster sugar
2 measures hot water
Add to glass, dissolve the sugar. Dust with nutmeg

Hopeless Case
1 measure sloe gin
1/2 measure peppermint schnapps
3 measures cold cola
Add to ice-filled glass. Garnish: lime slice

Best Year
1 measure vodka
1/2 measure blue curacao

1/2 measure Licor 43
11/2 measures pineapple juice
1/2 measure Rose's Lime Cordial
Shake and strain into glass filled with broken ice

Waste of Time
1 measure Midori
1 measure white rum
1/2 measure amaretto
2 measures pineapple juice
Prepare 2 glasses
Glass 1: rim with grenadine/caster sugar,add cherry on stick. Garnish: fruit in season.
 Glass 2: plain, ungarnished. Shake and strain into glass 2.
Serve both!

The Belchester Chronicles
by
Andrea Frazer

For more information about **Andrea Frazer**
and other **Accent Press** titles

please visit

www.accentpress.co.uk

Lightning Source UK Ltd.
Milton Keynes UK
UKOW06n1006051215

264051UK00001B/12/P